---- ★ ----

THE CROWD BRIGHTENED WITH ANTICIPATION

Maybe something was about to happen to justify their long, rainy vigil.

Two men stood near the center of the small square, engrossed in conversation. One of them, a short, grossly overweight man whose badge identified him as Sheriff Price, nodded at Boyd and gravely shook his hand before suspiciously growling, "Who are you?" at me. I bristled at his tone—Eileen always tells me I have a problem with authority figures; maybe she's right.

I didn't have time to answer. Boyd rushed to the center of the square and fell to his knees beside the blanketed corpse.

"Amanda?"

The blanket was pulled back to expose the bloody and battered face of Amanda Johnson, raindrops streaming from her face. Her once brilliant, expressive green eyes were wide open, surprised by death.

---- ★ ----

"Zukowski's pacing is good and her characterizations superb."

—*Publishers Weekly*

The
Hour
of the
Knife

SHARON ZUKOWSKI

W❀RLDWIDE.

TORONTO • NEW YORK • LONDON
AMSTERDAM • PARIS • SYDNEY • HAMBURG
STOCKHOLM • ATHENS • TOKYO • MILAN
MADRID • WARSAW • BUDAPEST • AUCKLAND

Grateful acknowledgment is made for permission to quote from the following:

"Cover Me" by Bruce Springsteen. Copyright© 1984 by Bruce Springsteen.

"Cheeseburger in Paradise," words and music by Jimmy Buffet. Copyright© 1978 by Coral Reefer Music & Outer Banks Music BMI.

"Blowin' in the Wind" by Bob Dylan. Copyright© 1962 by Warner Bros. Music; copyright© renewed 1990 by Bob Dylan. This arrangement copyright© 1992, Special Rider Music. All rights reserved. International copyright secured. Reprinted by permission.

Excerpts from the English translation of the *Rite of Funerals* copyright© 1970 by the International Committee on English in the Liturgy, Inc. All rights reserved.

Excerpts from the *New American Bible,* copyright© 1970 by the Confraternity of Christian Doctrine, Washington, D.C., are used with permission.

THE HOUR OF THE KNIFE

A Worldwide Mystery/July 1993

First published by St. Martin's Press, Incorporated.

ISBN 0-373-26123-3

Printed in U.S.A.

It is now or never, the hour of the knife.
The break with the past, the major operation.

—C. Day Lewis

PROLOGUE

Thursday

"THIS WHOLE WORLD is out there just trying to score. I've seen enough, I don't want to see any more." The hoarse voice thundering from the radio was a perfect reflection of my own dark mood. I lit another cigarette and turned the volume even higher.

I had left sunny Manhattan shortly after the morning traffic rush ended and had driven south into bad weather. Ten hours of driving over crowded, rain-soaked highways had not helped my disposition—I was tired and wanted a run, a long hot shower, and a quiet dinner. Most of all, I didn't want to be starting this vacation, but Eileen, my partner and older sister, had demanded that I get away. To be honest, she had thrown me out of the office. I remember her parting words, "Don't come back here for at least a month!" and scowled.

Eileen was wrong. I didn't need a vacation; I needed—what did I need? My mind could never fill in the blank; the sentence always ended unfinished.

My life fell apart two and a half years ago when my husband, Jeff, was murdered. I held the pieces together with a shaky combination of alcoholism and overwork. About six months ago, I realized that my destructive formula wouldn't work any longer. I stopped drinking and became a total workaholic. The only benefit of my new addiction was a profitable business. The brand-new Porsche I was driving, a recent gift to myself to celebrate a good year, was testimony to that. When Eileen and I started our business (I investigate, Eileen does the courtroom work), being profitable was the main priority. Otherwise, why bother? I could have been a staff investigator for an insurance company, Eileen a corporate attorney: Both come with nice salaries and good benefits.

But that didn't happen. Seven years ago, we sat at our family's annual Thanksgiving dinner complaining about our jobs and bosses. After graduating from law school, Eileen had gone to work for the Manhattan District Attorney. At the time, she had just left the D.A. to get on the partner track at a midtown law firm. I had done a tour with the NYPD before opening my own investigative agency. Tired of working alone, I soon joined the staff of a large agency. Agency work wasn't agreeing with me. I'd been assigned to matrimonial investigations—following sneaky husband and wives cheating on their spouses. It was hard to determine whose job was worse.

The brilliant idea hit at the same time. I put my fork down and looked across the table at Eileen.

"Why don't we—"

"—start a business?"

In the years we'd been together, we'd developed an impressive roster of clients: Wall Street firms wanting to learn more about employees before promoting them to lofty positions, banks worrying about the security of their fragile computer networks, and Fortune 500 companies with concerns too sensitive to be handled by their internal departments.

It's a clean business. We avoid the messy cases like divorce, checking out potential lovers, and locating missing family members. Everything was under control, until a few weeks ago. One of my cases ended abruptly when a forty-five-year-old broker, accused of defrauding her firm, committed suicide before I uncovered the evidence that implicated her assistant. Depression and guilt gave me an excuse to go back to drinking—that's when Eileen threw me out.

"Outside's the rain, the driving snow. I can hear the wild wind blow. Turn out the light. Bolt the door. I ain't going out there no more."

I squinted through the smoke-filmed windshield and watched my exit slide by. I cursed, but swerving across three lanes of interstate highway and backing up on the shoulder during the deluge wasn't a good idea. So I drove another ten miles to the next exit, made a U-turn and headed back. Not a great start to my vacation, but I didn't care; I was used to expecting the worst.

ONE

THIS WAS MY SECOND visit to Dolphin Beach, a small city on the Carolina coast, and while I was looking forward to seeing an old friend once again, I was also anxious to complete my business with her and forget about work for a while. Like any waterfront town in this country, Dolphin Beach was crammed with family resorts, cheap tourist motels, and staid hotels on the beach. I chose the Harbour House Inn, one of the oldest, quietest, and most expensive hotels on the water. The age, price, and view didn't interest me; I craved the quiet.

Registration was accomplished with a minimum of fuss; everything at the inn was accomplished with a minimum of fuss. I was about to leave the counter when the clerk stopped me. "Miss Stewart, you received several telephone calls. If you wait a minute, I'll get them for you." He disappeared through a door marked Employees Only and soon returned, four message slips in hand. They all had the same Manhattan telephone number, all were from my sister Eileen. All were marked, *"Urgent! Call as soon as possible."*

A bellhop led me to my suite. I followed, absent-mindedly snapping my fingers against the papers, wondering what had prompted Eileen's calls. After paying a ransom for my overnight bag, I kicked off my shoes, took one last look at the messages, crumpled them up into a tight little ball, and tossed it at the wastepaper basket. It bounced off the rim and landed in the center of the room.

Business could wait; I was on vacation. And if I delayed any longer, it would be too dark for me to enjoy the long run on the beach I had been promising myself all day long.

I rummaged through the suitcase seaching for my running clothes, ignoring the bright pink wad laying on the beige rug as well as the phone on the bedside table. I sat down on the bed, pulled on my running shoes, and looked at the ball on the floor. I even picked it up, bounced it in my palm, and considered making the call. Instead of picking up the telephone, I dropped the papers into the garbage can; they hit bottom with a satisfying thunk. I did a few half-hearted warm-up exercises and walked out to the beach without giving Eileen's calls another thought.

MY LONG, SLOW WORKOUT ended in a race against the rain clouds. The rain won. I was soaking wet and panting from the exertion by the time I reached the shelter of the hotel. But I was also feeling good—almost happy.

Running had worked its magic again; my faint smile had grown into a wide, silly grin. I peeled off my wet shorts and T-shirt and dropped them onto the bathroom floor. A very long, very hot shower was the next item on the list of treats I'd promised myself. I was about to step into the bathtub when the telephone rang. I hesitated.

Two rings. My smile faltered.

Three rings. I stood naked in the steamy bathroom, one foot in the tub, the other solidly planted on the tile floor, and tried to ignore the ringing telephone.

Four rings. My conscience won the battle. I grabbed a robe from the back of the door and shrugged into it. Five rings. And rushed into the bedroom.

Six rings. And picked up the telephone.

"Blaine?" I didn't have an opportunity to say more than hello. "They told me you checked in over an hour ago. Didn't you get my messages?"

I stretched out on the bed and stared at the ceiling. "Yes, I got your messages but I decided to go for a run first. Remember, I'm on vacation; the vacation you insisted I take. I don't care what the problem is, handle it yourself. Will you please leave me alone?"

A tiny spider journeyed across the ceiling, searching for an exit. I watched it sympathetically. Even though I realized I was acting like a jerk, I wasn't ready to forget the last argument Eileen and I had about my drinking; it was the fight that led to my forced vacation. I repeated, "I'm on vacation."

"Sorry to interrupt your precious vacation; this is important. It's business."

"Weren't you listening? I don't care. I'm in this crummy town because of business . . ."

"You told me Dolphin Beach was cute."

"Not when there's a tropical storm parked overhead, dumping inches of rain on the town." I gave up. "What's so damn important?"

"Boyd Johnson called this morning...."

"If he wants to postpone our meeting, call him back and tell him to forget it." I realized I was shouting and, with effort, lowered my voice. "Damnit, I'm not going to sit around and wait until he and Amanda can fit me into their hectic schedules. If they can't find the time to meet with me, I'll leave the report with their receptionist."

"Cut it out!" Eileen's voice sounded uncannily like the one our dad had used to break up our fights when we were kids. He had a great deal of practice; we fought a lot. Her voice softened as she said, "Listen, I wouldn't have bothered you if it wasn't important. Boyd needs your help. Amanda is missing."

"Police," I mumbled into the phone, suddenly too exhausted to say more.

"What did you say?"

It took a tremendous effort, but I found the energy to raise my voice. "Tell Boyd to call the police."

"He has. He asked for your help." Eileen's voice was slow and distinct, a sign of growing anger. "I told Boyd you would call him."

"Amanda has a horrible temper. They probably had a fight and she took off to cool down. It's nothing to worry about; she'll come back tomorrow, ready to forgive Boyd for whatever caused the argument. And I thought it was against our company policy to get involved in marital spats."

"And I thought you and Amanada were old college buddies; one of your best friends from school."

"Which is an even better reason not to get involved in their personal problems."

"You make me sick." The anger in Eileen's voice made me sit up and brace my feet on the carpet. "I'm tired of seeing everyone tiptoe around you, watching out for your foul moods, saying 'poor Blaine.' I know how hard things have been for you—I know better than anyone. But you're wallowing in self-pity." She stopped, afraid she had gone too far.

Eileen was right, but I wasn't ready to admit it. I sighed. "Okay, you win. I'll call Boyd, listen to his problems, and see if I can help."

She must have been sitting at her neat desk, holding her breath and nervously twisting the telephone cord around her finger. She said, "Great—keep me posted." We carefully skirted the real issues of the past month and said polite good-byes.

The last of my runner's euphoria disappeared while I dialed the Johnsons' phone number, listened to Boyd's brief explanation, and promised to get to their house as quickly as possible. The depression I had been fighting off rushed back over me. "I've seen enough. I don't want to see any more...."

I dumped the robe on the bed, pulled on jeans and a sweatshirt, and ran out, cursing the raincoat safely locked inside the car. I was soaked by the time I unlocked the door and dove in behind the wheel.

HARBOUR DRIVE, the town's main street, twisted away from the waterfront and into the business district. I drove past boutiques, gift shops, and restaurants before entering Dolphin Beach's historical Victorian district. Some of the dwellings had been restored to their former elegance, but most were still run-down, decaying in the salty air, silent proof that the benefits of tourist dollars hadn't trickled down to everyone.

I cursed those Victorians, they all looked the same to me—my eyes were more attuned to tall, city buildings. After several wrong turns, I found the Johnsons' house. It was a Victorian (what else?) but this one didn't have sagging porches, peeling paint, or hanging gutters; this house was in perfect condition.

Someone inside was waiting impatiently and pulled open the front door of the house before I finished parking. Boyd stood in the doorway and watched me hurry up the flagstone walk. Even in the dim porch lighting, I could see his anxiety.

He hung my dripping coat on a brass rack and silently led me to the kitchen. The house had been furnished with costly antiques and plush oriental rugs. The kitchen, filled with modern restaurant equipment, not a rickety antique in sight, was the only exception.

I leaned against the work station in the center of the room, ducking to avoid the copper pots dangling from the ceiling, and watched Boyd make coffee. He painstakingly ground beans and silently poured boiling water over the coffee. I was afraid to disturb his concentration, so I waited for the operation to be completed. He finally handed me a heavy mug of steaming coffee. I took a sip, attempted to roll it around my mouth mimicking a gourmet tasting a fine wine, and was disappointed. Boyd's creation didn't taste any better than the coffee I purchased every morning at the deli near my office. My taste buds had been destroyed by years of cardboard take-out coffee.

Boyd continued to ignore me, busying himself dumping wet grounds into the garbage disposal and wiping the gleaming counter. I leaned against the counter and tightened my grip on the mug, trying to remember the good intentions brought on by Eileen's lecture. But I was feeling cranky. I said, "You know, I didn't come out here for a cup of coffee. The hotel has a coffee shop and room service. I could have called them, had coffee delivered, and stayed dry. Now, what's the urgent problem?"

Rude, but it captured his attention. Boyd turned around and stared at his feet. "To tell you the truth, I'm not really sure there's a problem."

I gently put the blue mug down on the counter and said calmly, "Thanks for the coffee. I'm going back to my hotel to have a very late dinner. You can call me if you decide you need my assistance," and I started to walk out of the kitchen.

"Wait." Boyd grabbed my arm as I brushed past him. "I'm sorry, I'm a little upset...."

He held my arm in a tight, painful grip. I pried his fingers open and gently rubbed the skin. A red outline of his fingers shone on my skin; my arm would be black and blue in the morning. I looked at the mark and lost my temper. "Let's get one thing straight. I don't play games. You called me, left urgent messages about needing my help. Here I am. Tell me what's going on, why you so desperately need my help, or I'm leaving. And if you grab me like that again, I'll break your arm."

He recoiled and looked sheepish. "I'm sorry...I'm not thinking clearly. On Monday, Amanda and I had a fight in the office. Amanda stormed out. I stayed at the office, hoping she would cool off by the time I got home. She didn't. She left early the next day, around six, for a meeting in Wilmington. I guess she was still mad at me because she didn't wake me to say goodbye. You know how long Amanda can stay mad."

I nodded in agreement. In college, Amanda would get mad and not speak to me for days, until the anger worked itself out of her system.

Boyd continued. "She had meetings scheduled in Wilmington. She was going to come back Tuesday night. She never came home, she never called."

He stared at a mug, wondering how it had gotten into his hand. We both ignored the tears forming in his eyes; his voice fell to a harsh whisper. "I'm afraid something has happened to Amanda. I wish I had gotten up before she left...."

I opened the refrigerator door and pushed a few containers around, looking for the cream, giving Boyd time to regain control. "You called the police?"

"Yes." He shook his head. "I called yesterday around noon. The detective wasn't very helpful; he told me it was too early for them to do anything. I drove back and forth to Wilmington twice, hoping to find her car broken down on the side of the road. Nothing. I checked all the hospitals. Nothing. I called the police again today. They wrote up a missing persons report but haven't done anything else.''

Standard procedure, but people always expect more action from the police departments. Boyd went on. ''I called your office. I knew we had a meeting scheduled and that you would be in town. I talked to Eileen. She's your sister?''

I nodded, pulled a small notebook and pen from my pocketbook, and asked, ''What have the police done?''

''The same things I did. They checked the hotels and the hospitals and didn't find any sign of her. No one has seen Amanda since she left.''

We talked for another half an hour. I asked a lot of questions and didn't receive many answers. Amananda was missing. Boyd hadn't heard from her. I stifled a yawn and looked at my watch, thinking of the long, leisurely dinner I had missed, and said, ''It's late; I can't do anything tonight. Try to sleep, I'll call you in the morning.'' I edged to the door, hoping the hotel restaurant was still open.

Boyd followed, asking questions, seeking reassurance. I knew the right words, the ones that would make him feel better and let him sleep. And even though I wasn't convinced Amanda was in trouble—she was probably too pissed off to call Boyd—I couldn't say those comforting words. Maybe it was intuition; maybe I was too tired and too hungry to

linger; or maybe I was unable to play the role of com-
fort-giver anymore. The words used to flow with ease;
maybe I really needed this vacation.

I pulled my slicker from the rack and walked out
onto the porch. Boyd followed. I was standing on the
top stair with my back to the street, repeating my
promise to call in the morning, when he stiffened and
looked past me to the street.

I turned to watch a police car park behind my car.
My stomach sank; I understood the significance of this
late night visit. Boyd didn't. We watched a policeman
hurry up the walk.

"Mr. Johnson? I'm Officer Davis; the sheriff would
like you to come with me, sir." He paused, pulled his
hat off, and nervously cleared his throat before rushing on. "I'm sorry to tell you this, sir. We need you to
make an identification." The porch light wasn't bright
enough for me to see Boyd's face clearly or judge his
reaction. The sharp intake of breath I heard was mine.

Boyd said, "Identification? What do you mean?"

"It's your wife. We think we located her. I'm sorry,
sir, but she's dead. We need you to identify the body."

The men stared at each other. Davis twisted his hat
in his hands; Boyd ran his hand through his hair. Neither was sure of the next step. Boyd's lips moved; no
sound followed. I broke the silence and said to the
policeman, "Why don't we follow you in my car?"

Davis agreed, happy to be relieved of the responsi-
bility. Boyd dashed out into the rain to my car; I
grabbed his jacket from the rack, closed the door, and
slowly followed him.

We drove south, heading out of town on a two-lane road. Once outside the city limits, the police car picked up speed. I pressed harder on the accelerator; the Porsche had no trouble matching the pace of the car ahead.

Boyd and I were both silent, engrossed in our thoughts, watching the revolving blue light on the police car's roof. Boyd mumbled, "They made a mistake..." I clutched the steering wheel tighter and let his remark pass without comment; better to let him hang on to his hope a little while longer.

After ten agonizing miles, Davis slowed, signaled a left turn, and disappeared into a barely visible gap between the pine trees. The sandy lane was just wide enough for our cars. All my concentration was devoted to the narrow path. I maneuvered between the ruts and puddles, wincing as branches slapped against the brand new paint of my brand new car. Furious at myself for worrying about scratches, I turned my attention back to the road.

It seemed to be miles and miles, but the odometer had counted off only four-tenths of one when the police car stopped in a small, grassy clearing strewn with official-looking vehicles. We waited. Boyd continued to mutter, "Mistake..."

I rolled the window down. Davis stuck his head into the opening; raindrops streamed from the brim of his hat and landed in my lap. "There's too much muck up ahead for anything but a four-wheel drive to get through. Your car will never make it. We'll have to walk from here. It's not too far."

We formed a single-file parade. Davis led, Boyd went second, I lagged behind, not anxious to reach the end of the trail. Davis shone an inefficient flashlight on the path, then finally decided the light was useless and shoved it into a pocket. Before my eyes could adjust to the darkness, I stepped into a deep puddle. Water poured into my sneakers; I mumbled, "Shit," and kept walking.

We hiked between tall marsh reeds and low scrub pines, my feet squishing with each step. I managed to step into every puddle on that trail.

The path ended, blocked by Jeeps, sheriff department seals emblazoned on the doors. They faced a small clearing, headlights illuminating the area. We stepped around the cars; I reluctantly dragged behind the two men, not eager to be confronted with another too-familiar crime scene.

Yellow plastic tapes marked with large black letters spelling out POLICE LINE. DO NOT CROSS. outlined a tiny square patch of marsh grass. Two groups of people waited for action.

One group, the police, stood inside the ribbons, smoking cigarettes and quietly talking. Occasionally one would halfheartedly order a bystander to move back from the yellow ribbon; the rest of them ignored the second group that had gathered outside the tape.

They were the spectators, the ones who appear no matter how ghastly the scene or the weather. They patiently stood outside the clearing waiting for something exciting.

The crowd brightened wtih anticipation as we approached; maybe something was about to happen to justify their long, rainy vigil. I shuddered with contempt for the human vultures gathered around the corpse, waiting to feed on our grief. I wanted to shout out, "Go home; leave us alone!" I ignored them and ducked under the tape.

Two men stood near the center of the small square, engrossed in conversation. They stopped talking when Davis lifted the ribbon, and watched our approach. One of them, a short, grossly overweight man whose badge identified him as Sheriff Price, nodded at Boyd and gravely shook his hand before suspiciously growling, "Who are you?" at me. I bristled at his tone—Eileen always tells me I have a problem dealing with authority figures; maybe she's right.

I didn't have time to answer. Boyd rushed to the center of the square and fell to his knees beside the blanketed corpse. His voice quavered as he extended a trembling hand to touch the blanket. "Amanada?"

The blanket was pulled back to expose the bloody and battered face of Amanda Johnson, raindrops streaming from her face. Her once brilliant, expressive green eyes were wide open, surprised by death.

I wanted to cry out, to add my voice to Boyd's pitiful moan. "Oh God, it's Amanda..." But I didn't make a sound; the cool detached professional took over. Knowing I would pay later, I stood behind Boyd and forced myself to look at the body, burning the sight into my memory. After a few minutes we both had had enough. I put my arms around Boyd's shoulders and gently helped him to his feet.

The vultures stirred, circling for a better view of the grieving husband. I said, "For God's sake, can't you cover her or at least keep those people back?" The sheriff ignored my request. Boyd stared at Amanda, not reacting as the blanket covered her face. A policewoman detached herself from the small group of gossipers and ordered the crowd back. She caught my slight nod of thanks, grinned, and returned the nod. Only slightly mollified, I turned to the sheriff and asked, "How was she killed?"

"Shot. Not here—somebody drove back and dumped her into the swamp. Only, it don't look like she was dead when they dropped her. She clawed her way out of that marsh 'fore she died. Autopsy will tell us more. No one in those houses back there," he said as he gestured to a stand of pine trees behind us, "heard anything. That lady over there"—he pointed to a policeman who was standing apart from the flock of vultures quietly talking with a woman and making occasional notations in a small notebook—"her dog found the body. She let him out and he didn't come back when she called him. She went lookin' for him and found him sniffing around the body. She called us 'bout an hour ago."

"Tire tracks?"

The sheriff paused to rub the bald spot on the back of his head before answering my question. "None. I reckon the rain washed out any tracks. We'll take a closer look in the daylight." Price looked at Boyd and abruptly ended our discussion. "Ma'am, why don't you take Mr. Johnson on home now? No sense in making him stay out here in the rain any longer. I'll talk to him in the morning."

We walked back silently through the dark mist to the cars. I barely noticed the mucky puddles, even though I again managed to step in every one.

Amanda occupied my thoughts. Not the Amanda who had been abandoned in the muck, left to struggle out of the mud and die alone in the darkness, but the woman who had once been a close friend.

We had met during our freshman year in college. My fledgling academic career was being threatened by a basic computer class—I was failing it. The professor suggested, demanded, that I find a tutor. I found Amanda—a gifted, but not always patient, tutor—a passing grade, and a close friend.

During the next three years, we were inseparable: rooming together, studying together, double-dating, growing up together. After college ended we kept in touch through visits, phone calls, and long, gossipy letters. Gradually, without notice, we drifted off into separate lives. She returned to her southern home; I returned to my cherished New York City.

I would occasionally stumble across an old photo album and flip thorugh it, wondering about Amanda's life. For a fleeting moment I would think of using my professional contacts to locate Amanda, but never did. I've seen too many reunion scenes end in disillusionment and disappointment to get involved in one of my own. The reminiscing would always end

THE HOUR OF THE KNIFE 25

abruptly with the photo album being slammed shut and tossed to the floor.

Two months ago, a depressing Monday morning was brightened by an unexpected telephone call. The call also brightened Eileen's day—it brought business into our firm which was suffering from the summer blahs: everyone was on vacation, or planning one. No one wanted to do anything resembling work.

CIG, the Canfield Insurance Group, had recommended a complete review of the security procedures at BAJ Enterprises and had suggested our firm. Amanda was BAJ's president and cofounder, married to the company's chief executive officer. Amanda laughed. "You? Security? God help my company!"

Shortly after that conversation, we held a private reunion at the Dolphin Beach Regional Airport. This was the season of airport delays and my flight was not exempt—we landed forty-five minutes late. I hurried off, wrinkled and annoyed by the delay, apprehensive about meeting Amanda. I rushed past the tall, elegant woman who was leaning against a pillar near the gate coolly appraising each passenger, dropped my garment bag, and looked around.

The woman straightened up and said, "Blaine, aren't you going to say hello?" It was Amanda. Every brown hair perfectly placed, flawless makeup, a pale yellow linen suit unwrinkled and unaffected by the humidity. I walked beside her, feeling dowdy and awkward, even though my fears were unwarranted; after all, I was dressed in my best business clothes, every red curl in its place. Completely intimidated by her presence, I spent the few minutes it took to walk to the parking lot wondering if we would be able to discover any common ground to renew our friendship.

Later that evening we settled on the front porch with iced tea and cigarettes to enjoy the mild spring air. It was time to relax. The perfect suits were carefully hung in our respective closets, and I was feeling sheepish; I confessed my earlier doubts. Amanda bellowed with laughter and confided similar fears.

We sat until dawn talking, laughing, crying, rediscovering our friendship. And now I had come to town to deliver my final report.

BOYD WANTED TO BE left alone; in fact, he insisted on it. I parked the car and stubbornly followed him into the house.

It was my turn to make the coffee. Boyd slumped in a chair at the table, cradling his head in his hands as I fussed with the grinder and coffee beans. Maybe inattention is the secret of great coffee—my version tasted much better than the weak stuff Boyd had brewed earlier.

Boyd looked at the steaming mug I placed before him. The light touch of my hand on his shoulder roused him. He blinked and said, "Did you say something?"

"Was Amanda working on anything important? Something sensitive?" I wanted to make sense of her death; maybe the cause could easily be tracked back to work.

He shrugged. "I don't know. Amanda handled all the technical details. She didn't involve me in her projects; we have—had—a sharp division of labor. Amanda took care of the technical work. I handled the marketing and financial details. It was pointless for Amanda to explain her projects to me; I didn't have the time to understand the fine details." He stared at the cup and asked, "Do you think there might be a connection between work and ... what happened?"

I shrugged and said, "Maybe, maybe not. Either way, I'd like to take a look around her office. I might get lucky and find a connection."

He shook his head dubiously. "I don't see how; we don't get involved in any business that could trigger a murder. Trying to decipher Amanda's notes would be a waste of time."

A stubborn expression settled on my face. Boyd noticed it and hastily added, "Of course, you're the expert. I know better than to argue with an expert. Louise, Amanda's secretary, usually gets in around eight-thirty. Come anytime after that; I'll instruct her to give you complete access to Amanda's office and files."

I disregarded his unspoken command to leave. "Actually, I would like to go there tonight. If Amanda did stumble onto something, it can't wait until morning. Whoever killed her won't wait until business hours to retrieve that information. They'll go there tonight. What's a little breaking and entering after you've commited murder?"

I had another reason; one I didn't mention to Boyd. I wanted to get to Amanda's office before the police arrived and sealed off my only opportunity to look around. If I waited until morning, it would be too late—if it wasn't already too late.

Boyd wasn't swayed by my reasoning. He shook his head and said, "It's the middle of the night. You can't go up there alone. And if you're right, it won't be safe. You could walk in on the people who killed Amanda. No, you'll have to wait until morning."

I made one last attempt to convince him and gave up. I had just completed an extensive review of BAJ's security; getting in wouldn't be any trouble. After murder, what's a little breaking and entering?

THE RIDE THROUGH the deserted office park was eerie and made worse by my churning stomach. Massive, dark buildings towered over the wide, gently curving street. Most of those buildings were also dark during the day, built with speculator's dollars when tax write-offs were more important than the investment. The buildings were vacant; the gamble had not yet paid off. The investors didn't care, their tax breaks and their buildings long forgotten.

BAJ Enterprises was located in one of those new buildings. A building personally financed by Boyd and Amanda, not the tax-dodging ploy of a rich man, or so Boyd had proudly informed me during a tour of the complex.

In bright sunlight, the buildings were forlorn and showed signs of neglect; the darkness made them spooky. I reined in my imagination and carefully parked in the shadows behind BAJ's office, hiding the car from the casual glance of a passing patrol.

The report I was supposed to deliver in the morning stressed the need for improvement in items as basic as locks. It was easy to pry open a rear door with a screwdriver from my tool kit—no one had heeded my advice to install a more secure lock.

The glow from the exit signs provided enough light to navigate the hallways to Amanda's office without any difficulty. Once inside, I carefully closed the door and made sure the drapes were tightly closed before turning my flashlight on her desk.

Files, memos, and computer printouts littered the desk top; they were piled in haphazard stacks, defying gravity and threatening to topple over at any moment. After a long period of time spent picking up files and rapidly scanning them, I gave up in frustration and turned to the drawers.

I pulled open the top drawer and found a crumpled pack of cigarettes. They weren't my usual brand but since mine were safely locked in the car, I couldn't be choosy. I lit one, pulled open the bottom drawer, propped up my feet, and leaned back in Amanda's comfortable leather seat to think.

Rumbles from my stomach interrupted my cigarette break, reminded me of a missed dinner, and urged me to stop wasting time thinking and hurry. Thoughts of coffee and sandwiches prompted a cursory search of another drawer. Nothing. I tried another drawer. Nothing. I looked through the bottom drawer. Nothing. I put my feet back up and took another deep drag on the cigarette.

This visit was pointless; my intuition had been wrong. I knew too much about the projects Amanda was working on and nothing about why she had been killed. I swung my feet to the floor and kicked the drawer shut, angry that my hunch had turned out to be another stupid idea. A stack of files wavered and plunged to the floor.

"Damn!" I ground the cigarette out in an ashtray and scrambled around on the floor to pull the papers together. The thin beam of light from my flashlight shone on a pocket-sized diary with a battered leather cover. I fished it out and stared at it; my fingers idly traced the gold initials on the maroon cover. A.M.G. Amanda Marie Griffin. I sat cross-legged on the floor, surrounded by the spilled papers, and gently cradled the journal. And I cried.

Amanda had discovered the miracle of time management during our senior year in college. All year long I listened to sermons on the benefits of organization and the value of planning. She never converted me to her system; I was happy to let my time pass unorganized.

My graduation present to Amanda had been a personalized daily organizer, one small enough to be tucked into a pocket, briefcase, or stack of papers. One with a maroon leather cover, stamped in gold with her initials. The one resting in my lap.

I stuck the little book into my pocket and finished picking up the files. After one last check of the office to be sure I wasn't leaving any sign of my visit, I made my way out to the car.

It was almost one o'clock in the morning. I was tired, too keyed up to sleep and very, very hungry. It was too late for room service; every restaurant and fast-food joint I passed was dark and tightly locked up for the evening. I drove past an all-night supermarket, and remembering the tiny kitchenette in the hotel suite, decided to stop for coffee and a late-night snack.

The shopping didn't take long; not many people were searching for groceries in the middle of the night. I made my purchases and drove back to the inn. The parking lot was crowded; I had to settle for a spot between a battered pickup truck and an even more battered van instead of the isolated parking spots I usually pick.

The car would get scratched—but not during the first month I owned it. I laughed at myself for being overprotective and bent down to grab the bag of groceries and my briefcase when I heard a noise behind me. I started to turn, but wasn't fast enough; something hard and unyielding crashed into the back of my head. A thousand light bulbs exploded inside my skull, instantly followed by darkness.

A HARSH LIGHT sliced through my eyelids; my head throbbed. When I tried to move away from the glare, a round, hard object cut into my cheek. I was cold and wet and stupidly realized I was lying on the damp gravel parking lot, stones beneath my cheek. Voices and other noises slowly filtered through the throbbing. A hand touched the back of my neck. I struggled to sit up; another strong hand easily held me down. A quiet voice said, "Don't fight; I'm a doctor. You're going to be fine. Just lie still; the ambulance will be here in a minute or two and then we'll go take some X rays and put in a few stiches."

I kept my eyes tightly closed against the sharp light and mumbled into the gravel, "Stitches?"

"Don't worry. It doesn't look serious."

"Ma'am?" Another, vaguely familiar voice spoke. "I'm a police officer. Can you tell me what happened?"

We must have looked ludicrous: a woman lying face down in a puddle, a doctor trying to stick Band-Aids on her head while a cop stood nearby asking, "What happened? What happened?"

Instead of laughing, I once again mumbled into the gravel, "Can this wait?"

"Davis." The doctor spoke with quiet authority. "You'll have to wait. Let's get this lady to the hospital. You can ask all the questions you want after I'm done."

I didn't want to go to a hospital. Both men ignored my protests. The doctor wasn't used to having his orders questioned, the cop was used to following orders, and my head hurt too much to argue. I meekly submitted to stretchers, ambulances, and my own flock of staring vultures.

The next hour and a half passed in a blur of forms, stitches, X rays, and questions. The doctor unwillingly released me after I solemnly promised to make his office my first stop in the morning.

In spite of my inability to answer his questions, Davis graciously drove me back to the inn and escorted me into my suite. He waited outside the door until the lock clicked shut. I listened to his footsteps disappear down the hallway, checked the lock again, and made my way to bed.

It was 4:00 A.M., long past the time I had planned to be asleep. I added my damp, soiled clothes to the growing pile in the bathroom and stumbled into the bedroom. I eased my aching body into the bed and instantly fell asleep.

TWO

Friday

THE SHRILL PEALING of the telephone woke me. During the night my headache had escalated from simple throbbing to severe pounding. I didn't want to move, fearful that movement would intensify the pain. But the ringing sliced like a knife through my closed eyes to the back of my head, each chime stabbing deeper and deeper; moving couldn't possibly hurt worse. I rolled over, grabbed the phone, and answered it with a curse that ended in a soft groan.

It was Eileen, sounding much too cheerful. Like most early risers, she has little tolerance for those of us who, even under the most favorable circumstances, find it impossible to function before ten o'clock in the morning. I, on the other hand, have absolutely no tolerance for those happy morning people. Eileen and I usually have our most heated fights early (by my standrds) in the morning.

My voice was hoarse from a lack of sleep. I croaked out, "Hi—what time is it?"

"Seven-thirty. What's wrong? You sound awful."

"Awful is an accurate description of how I feel. I didn't get to bed until after four." I discovered the thumping in the back of my head lessened if I lay very still. I concentrated on not moving; the throbbing eased. I took advantage of the quietness inside my head and said, "It was a busy evening. The police located Amanda; she's dead." I ignored Eileen's gasp and gave her a sketchy outline of the previous night's events.

My vivid imagination was busy as I talked. A vision of Amanda, weakly pulling herself from the dank muck, kept floating before my eyes. Despite my initial unwillingness, I was involved and would remain involved until the end.

The vision wouldn't go away. I ended by telling Eileen, "... and to add a truly exciting finish, I got mugged in the hotel parking lot." I omitted the details of my trip to Amanda's office and felt a twinge of guilt; I knew what Eileen's response would be and her sermon would only bring my headache back.

Eileen's three short words, "Are you okay?" conveyed both suspicion and concern. It was a question she had asked with increasing frequency during the past few months.

"I'm fine. I need more sleep. A few groceries, my old briefcase, and a stack of old magazines are gone. I have a couple scratches and a few stitches: nothing serious." My fingers absentmindedly strayed to the back of my head and made contact with the bandage. I winced and said, "I'm going to see the doctor who stitched me up later this morning, just to be sure my hard head is going to survive."

"I'm not trying to lecture you." Eileen cautiously selected her words; she knows how lecture-resistant I can be. "But please be careful...." I didn't pay much attention to her after that opening and tuned back in when Eileen said, "Blaine, you have a few messages here. Jona, your ever-efficient secretary, left them on my desk."

Eileen flipped through the messages and called them off. "Let's see...I can take care of this one.... He can wait.... She can wait.... Someone else can handle this." Her voice grew sharper. "Amanda Johnson called you Monday, late afternoon. I guess you had already left. No message—she just asked you to return the call. Wonder what she wanted?"

"Who knows? Who cares?" It didn't matter. We said our good-byes and hung up.

I tried to sleep, but the image of Amanda's body kept floating inside my eyelids. A few minutes later I gave up, shuffled into the bathroom, and looked in the mirror. A ghastly face looked back at me. Three hours of restless sleep produced a hangover worse than any evening of hard drinking ever did. My head hurt; red streaks of lightning ran through my eyes. My hair stuck out at odd angles; I was sweaty and felt dirty. Years of experience taught me I'd feel better if I could get my creaky body in motion.

A long, hot shower and several cups of strong black coffee improved my spirits but didn't ease the aches. I dressed slowly and left. I was halfway down the outside stairway, wondering how Southern people coped with humidity before air-conditioning, when my right hand strayed and pressed against the bandage, reminding me I wasn't fully dressed.

I ran back to the suite and pulled a battered aluminum case from the top shelf of the bedroom closet. It
only took a few seconds to unlock the case; I wasted
several more minutes staring at the contents.

A black, custom-fitted, .45 caliber, automatic pistol was nestled in a protective foam carrier. For
months at a time I forget about the gun; it stays locked
in the case, hidden from sight. Once or twice a year, I
find myself in peculiar circumstances that compel me
to bring it out. Every time I open that case, I stare at
the dark, ugly pistol, surprised to find myself in pos-
session of such a lethal object. I'm always reluctant to
touch it, fearful of the consequences if forced to un-
leash its deadly power.

The gun had been an odd, last-minute addition to
my luggage. In spite of my aversion, I was glad I'd
listened to the soft, inner voice when it insisted I pack
the automatic.

The soft leather holster was in the bottom of a suitcase. I slipped it on, tucked the pistol into its cradle,
and shrugged my way into a linen jacket; everything
was invisible under the jacket. I went outside, prepared to face the day and Dolphin Beach.

LAST NIGHT in the emergency room, after I remained
steadfast in my refusal to be admitted to the hospital—"Overnight, for observation"—the doctor rudely
thrust his card into my hand, mentioned early office
hours, and stalked out of the small cubicle where the
paramedics had deposited me. I looked at the card.

Hugh Reynolds, M.D., 315 Broad Avenue. It wouldn't be hard for a trained detective like me to find him.

The door to 315 Broad Avenue was unlocked, the lobby empty. Maybe eight-fifteen was too early. I called "Hello," and walked into the room.

A male voice answered my second, less tentative call. "I'll be with you in a few minutes. Make yourself comfortable."

The waiting room was filled with the standard furniture, computer crafted prints, a few plants, newspapers, and magazines. Boring—I didn't have any desire to snoop around. I decided to follow the doctor's advice and made myself comfortable on the sofa and picked up the morning edition of the local newspaper. A large photograph was prominently featured on the front page, providing cheap thrills for the readers. One of the circling vultures in the night had been equipped with a camera and captured the moment when I put my arms around Boyd's shoulders and helped him to his feet. Amanda's uncovered body was clearly visible in the foreground; grief etched deep lines on our faces.

Anger and the feeling of having been violated by the curious lens bubbled in my chest. Sometimes it's difficult for me to balance the public's right to be informed with a person's right to privacy; this was one of those times. I folded the paper, tossed it on the table, and tried to forgive the photographer for doing a job.

The tiny, self-righteous Thank You For Not Smoking sign on the table was the only reason why I didn't light a cigarette and puff away in disgust. Since smoking was outlawed, I leaned back, closed my eyes, and told myself to relax. It worked—I fell asleep.

A HAND TOUCHED my shoulder. I jumped, instinctively reaching for the pistol before my eyes were completely open. Fortunately, I opened them before I withdrew my hand, and gun, from beneath my jacket.

The doctor was sitting next to me, concern in his eyes; he was not accustomed to finding patients sleeping in the waiting room. I meekly followed him down a short hallway to an examining room, thankful that my reactions were slowed by three hours of sleep. Dr. Reynolds probaby considered patients waving guns in the waiting room even more unacceptable than sleeping ones.

The examination didn't take long. Reynolds busied himself checking reflexes, blood pressure, and stitches; while he occupied himself with medical matters, I made my own examination. Hugh Reynolds, M.D., was a very attractive man. Late thirties, at least six inches taller than my own 5'11", sandy hair with a few gray streaks, deep green eyes, and a wonderfully bushy mustache.

We were on a first-name basis before the examination was finished. Reynolds rattled off a long list of warning signs and cautionary advice. "The stitches will dissolve. I had to shave a little patch of hair on the back of your neck, but don't worry, it doesn't show. Your hair is long enough to cover it. In fact, your hair absorbed a lot of the force of the blow and probably saved you from a concussion. You should be fine, just don't get hit on the head again for the next few weeks. Now, you look a little tired—"

I've heard the speech he was getting ready to deliver many times before and didn't want to listen to it again, so I interrupted, "Can you blame me? It was a long night."

Reynolds laughed, pulled a prescription pad from the pocket of his lab jacket, and said, "No, can't say that I can blame you. Let me write you a prescription—guaranteed you'll feel better."

"Unless you're writing a prescription for six or seven hours of uninterrupted sleep, I'm not interested. I don't want drugs." I was also disappointed by his casual eagerness to write a quick-fix prescription.

He ripped the slip from the pad and handed it to me. "Doctor's orders."

I glanced at the paper, curious to see which tranquilizer he favored. A little Valium maybe? The surprisingly neat handwriting read, "Dinner. 7 P.M. The Caribbean Room, Harbour House Inn. Casual dress." I smiled and looked at him. He said, "Well?"

I laughed and said, "Nice work, Doc. You're right, I do feel better. My faith in the medical profession has been restored."

DAYLIGHT TRANSFORMED the corporate park from a spooky, deserted movie set to an ordinary, would-be center of commerce. The glass-walled buildings lost their menacing appearance and merely looked empty and forlorn. BAJ Enterprises was one of the few active spots in the development. It's parking lot was jammed with cars; I had to search for a space where I could safely park the Porsche.

The receptionist was busy gossiping on the telephone. I signed the visitor's log and glared at her, impatiently tapping the pen on the counter.

The woman wasn't fazed by my show of impatience. She calmly finished her conversation, flashed a toothy smile, and told me, "Mr. Johnson is expecting you. He's in a meeting right now and will be with you as soon as he is finished. He said you should make yourself comfortable." She dismissed me with another smile and turned her attention back to the switchboard.

Several men and women sat on leather sofas in the vestibule, waiting for their appointments, leafing through business journals, and sneaking glances at their watches. I didn't join them, afraid I would fall asleep if I stopped moving. Large photo murals, depicting the company's history, hung on the lobby walls. I paced in front of those photos, trying to sort out last night's events. A picture of the ground-breaking ceremony caught my eye. I stopped for a closer look; the photographer froze Amanda and Boyd clasping a shovel, proudly smiling as they scooped out the first clump of dirt, officially beginning the excavation. The next photo showed them standing hand in hand, watching a backhoe rake the ground.

I was absorbed by the pictures and wasn't aware of Boyd until he stood at my side. His face was haggard and drawn; he too had spent a sleepless night. Boyd murmured a greeting and said, "Sheriff Price is in my office; I need to spend a few more minutes with him. When he's done, I'll take you to see Louise and show you Amanda's office."

I smiled, assumed the most innocent expression I could dig up from my inventory, and said, "Don't worry, take your time. I'll go get a cup of coffee."

Boyd disappeared around the corner. I watched him and then hurried to Amanda's office—I knew the way—hoping no one was guarding the door. The receptionist didn't bother to look up from the phone as I walked past. My meager luck held; Louise was the only person in Amanda's outer office.

Suspicious, red-rimmed eyes looked at me. She said, "Can I help you? Oh, Miss Stewart, I'm sorry. I forgot to cancel your appointment. . . . I guess you didn't hear . . ." Her voice faltered then broke. Tears overflowed her eyes and streamed down her cheeks.

She fruitlessly searched her pockets for a tissue. I found a small pack in my purse and handed it to her. While she wiped her glasses and blew her nose I said, "Louise, I know. I was with Mr. Johnson last night when the police came." I shook my head, trying to shake the vision of Amanda's body from my mind. Louise's eyes filled with tears again. I rushed on to avoid another onslaught. "I need to look around Mrs. Johnson's office. Mr. Johnson gave me permission. He would have come himself but he's busy with the sheriff."

Louise didn't make any effort to stop me, but nodded, grabbed a memo from the top of her desk and carefully studied it. I was feeling too guilty about taking advantage of her grief to point out to her that the paper was upside down. By the time I crossed the room to Amanda's large walnut desk, all my guilty feelings were gone. Time was too short to waste on guilt.

I sat down behind the desk and went back to the stacks of files; maybe I had overlooked something important under last night's flashlight beam. Fifteen or twenty minutes passed before my headache returned, induced by technical jargon I didn't understand and technical charts that didn't make sense.

A cigarette would help. I pulled open the bottom drawer of the desk, which I knew would make an excellent footrest, propped up my feet, and lit a cigarette. Smoke swirled out into the air. I watched it curl into blue gray ribbons and started a list of my investigation's results. It was a short list: three stitches and a headache—great results.

The cigarette burned down to the filter. I stabbed it out and lit another one. I like to smoke when I brood, but this cigarette didn't provide any solace. Sitting around, brooding, smoking cigarettes wasn't the answer; it was time for action. I angrily mashed the cigarette into an ashtray, swung my feet down, and kicked the drawer shut.

It wouldn't close. I kicked it again and then got down on my knees to see what was blocking the drawer. The culprit was a small manila envelope standing up in the track. The office door slammed open just as my fingers touched the envelope.

Sheriff Price strode into the room and yelled, "Who the hell are you? And what are you doing in here?" Louise followed, meekly protesting.

I pulled the envelope free, stuffed it into my pocket, and scrambled to my feet—all in one smooth movement. I smiled, extended my hand, and innocently said, "Sheriff Price, good morning. Boyd never introduced us last night; my name is Blaine Stewart—"

He ignored my outstretched hand and said, "Listen, young lady."

"My name is—"

"I don't care what your name is. What the hell are you doing? You got no business here."

I was mad at myself for getting caught and said the first feeble thing that came to mind. "I'm waiting for Mr. Johnson."

"What's going on here?" Boyd stood in the doorway, Louise nervously fidgeting behind him. "John, will you stop shouting?" He looked at me and angrily said, "Blaine, what are you doing here? I thought you were going for coffee."

Price answered first. He sputtered and said, "She's interfering with police business, that's what she's doing. And if she don't stop meddling in official business, she's gonna be in real trouble."

My temper erupted. I turned to Price. "If you have a problem with me, talk to me. I'm not meddling in anything. I'm a private investigator and have been working with Boyd's company. And quit calling me 'she.' I told you my name!"

Boyd snapped, "Stop it," and cut off the angry response Price was beginning to form. "Is this going to help Amanda?" Boyd realized he was yelling, stopped, and glared at us.

Price spoke first. "Boyd, I am truly sorry. We're all riled up this morning. I reckon none of us got much sleep last night. Miz Stewart, ma'am, forgive me. There's no excuse for my bad manners."

The tone of his voice negated the apology, taunting me to respond. Given more favorable circumstances, I would have replied, but not today. The envelope was burning through my pocket. I nodded and sidled to the door.

"Miz Stewart?" The sheriff's soft voice stopped me. "You haven't removed anything, have you? Surely you know that would be tampering with evidence." The threat in his voice was unmistakable.

Rules sometimes need to be broken and one or two big ones had fallen during the past twelve hours. Escape was my only reason for living at the moment. I looked directly into Price's eyes and lied. "No sir." I shook my head. "I sat behind her desk and smoked a cigarette. I hoped it would make me feel closer to her, help me understand what happened...."

He didn't believe me but couldn't prove I was lying. He said, "You know tampering with evidence is a serious offense."

I didn't wait to hear the warning. I walked out of the room, the envelope smoldering in my pocket. Boyd followed, torn between apologizing for the scene and berating me for causing it. I invented an excuse and fled the building after making arrangements to meet Boyd later in the afternoon.

The ride to town was nerve-racking. I continually checked the mirrors, expecting to see a police car in pursuit. None followed but I kept checking and relaxed only after I reached the safety of the hotel, the door securely locked and chained.

I stripped off my jacket, gun and holster, tossed them on the bed, kicked off my shoes, and walked out onto the balcony, turning the envelope in my hands. The beach was crowded with families enjoying the summer sunshine, trying to hurry their suntans before tropical storm Hannah reappeared.

I sat above the happy tourists, ripped open the envelope, and pulled out a series of spreadsheets. They showed the financial condition of an unnamed family for the past five years. These people—I could only assume they were Boyd and Amanda—were in serious trouble. My untrained eye quickly tallied expenses greatly exceeding income and noted colossal debts. Each year the debts grew larger, and the cash flow shrank until the family was close to insolvent. I threw the sheets down on the table and massaged my throbbing head.

The diary! I jumped up and ran to the bathroom. Fortunately the efficient housekeeping service didn't include picking up dirty clothes; they were still in a damp pile near the bathtub. I rummaged through the heap of clothes, picked up the sweatshirt I was wearing the night before, looked at the bloodstain on the collar, and tossed it aside. The jeans were on the bottom of the pile, untouched, the diary still in the back pocket.

The telephone rang; I got up from the cool tile floor and rushed to answer it. It was Eileen. She said hello and got to work. Eileen doesn't make small talk during business hours. "I've got some information for you. I checked into the Johnsons' background. Nothing unusual, the American Dream come true."

The spreadsheets were fresh in my mind. I asked, "Did you get a credit report?"

"No, but I will. Have you met with Boyd?"

"I tried but had a disagreement with the local sheriff and decided to leave." Dropping that little bit of information was a mistake. Eileen would jump all over me. "I'm scheduled to see Boyd later this afternoon."

She didn't disappont me; her response was predictable. "You'd better be careful. It's going to be difficult for me to bail you out if you manage to get yourself into trouble with the police again. You're not in New York now; I don't have any connections down there to help if you get yourself arrested again."

Eileen goes to bed early. She hates midnight calls requesting her presence at some precinct where I'm waiting for an attorney who can reason with an angry cop who arrested me for poking around in his business. It's not that I have a habit of getting arrested, it's an occupational hazard.

"Thanks, Eileen. I appreciate your support. The episode to which you're referring wasn't my fault."

·Eileen snorted, "You were arrested—somebody thought it was your fault."

My last dreadful case ended with my arrest. The charge: murder. I got to my client minutes after she had killed herself. The cops were close behind, they found me standing over her body. Thinking they had a neat solution to the crime, they arrested me. Eileen was the recipient of another late-night call to bail me out.

"You're not being fair. You know that was a misunderstanding. The sheriff and I had a little disagreement. It wasn't serious." It was time to change the subject before Eileen probed for the reason behind the little disagreement. Eileen, the attorney, doesn't always agree with my methods. We've had several major fights on the subject; I didn't want to start another.

Eileen and I work well together. When the tension builds to the point of being unbearable, we go into the conference room (it's important to be on neutral ground), firmly close the door, and refuse to accept any interruptions. We yell and scream at each other, cool off, come up with a solution, and get back to work, the discord forgotten. It was unusual for Eileen to pick at a past mistake. I thought for a few seconds and said, "Something's bothering you. What else is wrong?"

"Canfield Insurance called this morning. They want us to investigate Amanda's murder."

"Was CIG handling their life insurance?"

"Yes." Eileen's monotone was carefully nonjudgmental. "Business and personal coverage. The Johnsons recently made a dramatic increase in the face value of their policies. CIG wants us to investigate before they settle."

I didn't want to ask, but I did. "How much of an increase?"

"The total amount of insurance on Amanda's life is five and a half million dollars."

Eileen waited for a response. "Well, it's been done before," was all I could think of saying.

"Did you agree to work for Boyd on this?"

"No, I've just been tagging along, sticking my nose into things."

"Good. You'll have to inform Boyd that we have a client."

"I'll talk to him this afternoon. He won't be pleased."

Springsteen's lyrics, "I've seen enough. I don't want to see any more," rang through my head. All the weariness I had been trying to run away from came back and engulfed me. Too many killings, too much betrayal, too much greed. It was time for a run; I didn't care if the jarring brought my headache back.

I hid the papers and the diary and eagerly changed into running clothes. Unlike a lot of joggers who complain about the boredom of running and endure it only for the benefits of exercise, I love to run. Long runs keep me physically and, more importantly, mentally fit. I went out to the beach and ran, ignoring the swimmers, sunbathers, and the children building sand castles; not thinking, enjoying the movement and the warmth of the sun. The lethargy disappeared after five or six hard miles; I turned back to the hotel and tried to overlook the storm clouds gathering offshore.

HARBOUR DRIVE IS filled with restaurants. I searched for one that didn't have fishnets hanging in the windows or fish mounted above the doorway and finally, reluctantly, settled on one promising "Kountry Cooking." In spite of my misgivings about violating my personal dining rule #1: "The cuter the name, the worse the food," I went inside.

The decor wouldn't win awards, but the people crowded into the tiny cafe didn't care about the dingy interior. They were too busy gulping down food from overloaded plates to notice the grimy floors and walls. Battered chairs and tables, covered with paper placemats and illustrations of the fish found in local waters, were scattered around the room. I spotted a booth near the back of the room and headed for it. I wanted privacy, not a harbor view.

The waitress, a no-nonsense teenager, put a plastic glass of ice cubes in front of me, walked away, and returned carrying two pitchers of iced tea. She asked, "Regular or no sugar?" I opted for no sugar. I was learning that the regular version would be sweet enough to cause a mouthful of cavities. Each time the glass was empty, she instantly refilled it without comment. The meal, a fried fish sandwich, hush puppies, a homemade slaw, compensated for the paper plates, plastic utensils, and run-down interior.

I was making entries on my to-do list and enjoying one last cigarette when I looked up to see Sheriff Price approaching. I could feel a good case of indigestion starting. He nodded, said hello to the people who called out to him, but kept walking to my quiet corner.

He stopped next to the booth, tipped his hat and said, "Miz Stewart. Sorry to interrupt your lunch, ma'am. Mind if I sit a minute?" He squeezed his bulky frame into the booth without waiting for my answer. The waitress appeared and placed a glass of tea in front of him before he was completely settled. We were both silent as she removed my dirty plate and wiped the table.

Price placed his hat on the table between us. I leaned back against the red cushions and lit another cigarette. I tried to ignore the irrational hostility I felt toward, and from, this man and took a deep breath. I'm not good at making apologies, but I was operating in unfamiliar territory and couldn't alienate any potential source of information.

Eileen would have been proud of me. I smiled and said, "Sheriff, I would like to apologize for my behavior this morning. You were trying to do your job and I shouldn't have been in that office."

Price nodded and said, "No need for you to make pretty speeches. Like I said this morning, we were both a little riled up.... Boyd told me you and Mrs. Johnson were friends. He also said you're a private inves-tigator." His Southern drawl deepened, the gracious manner disappeared, and he asked, "You working for him?"

"No. My client is Canfield Insurance Group. CIG has underwritten the Johnsons' life insurance poli-cies; it's standard for them to request an investigation before settling such a large claim. We would appreci-ate your department's cooperation."

"You should know better than to meddle in police business. If you try to get in my way again, you'll be sorry."

I held up my hand and said, "Wait a minute—I'm supposed to be on vacation. All I want to do is file a report with the insurance company and get on with my trip. I have no desire to meddle in your business."

A broad smile spread across Price's face; he pulled a red bandanna from a hip pocket and wiped sweat from his forehead. Large, dark stains marked his khaki uniform; the air-conditioning was losing its battle against the humidity. He examined the ban-danna, stuffed it back into the pocket, and said, "Okay, ma'am, I just want to be sure we understand each other." He plucked his hat from the table, firmly settled it over the bald spot on the top of his head, and maneuvered his expansive body from the booth. "Stop by headquarters in a day or two, I'll let you have a look at the reports. Anything to speed you on your vacation."

"I DON'T BELIEVE IT! I thought you were Amanda's friend, my friend too. How could you do this? Of course I expected to hear from Canfield." Boyd's reaction was worse than I had imagined. I sat back and listened to him. "You're supposed to be a friend—but you dare to come in here and accuse me of murdering my wife for insurance money. I ought to throw you the hell out of here!" Bitterness spewed out across the desk. I opened my eyes and saw Boyd rise to his feet. I moved too, not wanting to give him an opportunity to carry out the threat.

Although I'd smoked too many cigarettes during the past two days, I'm in great physical condition and not afraid of threats. I also have a great deal of common sense. Common sense told me that Boyd, who outweighed me by fifty or sixty solid pounds, would be a tough match.

"Calm down." I spoke softly, trying to defuse his anger. "No one is accusing you of murder; these questions are standard. Yelling at me or trying to fight me won't do either of us any good. Why don't we try to work together?" We were on our feet, glaring at each other across the desk. "If I thought you murdered Amanda, I wouldn't be here talking with you; I'd be out digging up evidence to lock you up for the rest of your life. I'm on your side. Help me out, please."

Boyd collapsed into the chair, his anger deflated. I gratefully sank into the other chair. He stared at the desk and said, "It seems like I'm always saying 'I'm sorry' to you, but . . ."

"There's no need to apologize. I understand the strain you're under. Just remember, I'm on your side."

"Sure you are." The bitterness returned to Boyd's voice; the short truce was over. "What do you want?"

He was too angry, not at me but at the situation, to provide any useful information. I talked softly, trying to soothe him. "Boyd, I know what you're going through. Two days ago your life was perfect. Business was good, so was your marriage. You were happy. Suddenly, your happy life has been disrupted. No, it's been destroyed. And you don't know why it's happened. It's as if a terrorist tossed a bomb into the middle of your house and blew everything into tiny pieces while you stood by watching helplessly. I understand..."

"Yeah, you understand. Everybody understands. Fuck all you understanding people, you don't understand shit."

"I understand more than you think...." I lit a cigarette, took a deep drag, and we watched the smoke drift to the ceiling. My smoking was turning into a pack-a-day habit. I inhaled deeply and knew I would feel it during tomorrow's run. I took another deeper drag and drifted off into thought.

Jeff, my husband, and I met shortly after my graduation from college. It was love at first sight, for him, not for me....

Boyd looked at me, a puzzled expression on his face. I took one last puff on the cigarette and started talking again, smiling to hide my unsteady emotions.

"It's a cliché—one you've heard a million times today—but it's true, time will help. You won't ever completely lose the pain, but time will make that pain less intense." Or so I hoped, I added silently, avoiding the question in my mind: How much time would it take?

Some emotion in my face, or voice, touched Boyd. He said, "Okay, let's try it again. What do you need to know?"

His cool restraint didn't last long. My first question made him livid; he shouted, "Goddamnit! Yes, we increased our life insurance. Yes, it was a sizable increase. Doesn't that damn company read its own reports? Didn't they bother to tell you they approved the increase? Or that our accountant recommended the increase?"

I wanted to believe him—I needed to believe him—but I also had to check his story. I asked, "Who's your accountant?" And I would check, with or without Boyd's permission.

"Hollis Wilson. Jennifer can give you his number. I'll tell her to call him so he won't be surprised by your ridiculous questions. What else do you want?"

Even though I was afraid my response would push him completely over the edge of reason, I answered, "An employee list with their home addresses and telephone numbers," and braced for the explosions.

None came. Boyd smiled, picked up the telephone, issued a brief set of instructions, hung up, and said, "You'll have your list in fifteen or twenty minutes. I have work to do; you can wait outside."

I NEEDED A CUP of coffee. Jennifer cracked her gum and carefully considered my request to deliver the list in the cafeteria before answering, "Yeah sure. I can bring it to you there. Can ya wait about half an hour or so? I got some other work to do first."

"Sure." I went off to the cafeteria. Whoever named the room was either prone to exaggeration or had a weird sense of humor. BAJ clearly did not encourage its employees to waste valuable company time enjoying lunch or coffee breaks. The cafeteria was a small room with a few tables and orange plastic chairs crammed around them. "Food" could be purchased from machines in the corner.

At least the coffee appeared to be fresh. I filled a BAJ mug and sat on one of the neon chairs. My suspicions were confirmed. The company did not want people to linger; the chair was ugly, hard, and uncomfortable.

I exercised great self-control and didn't give in to the urge to light another cigarette but amused myself by staring at the safety posters decorating the walls. I heard hesitant footsteps in the doorway and turned to the entrance. It was Louise, standing in the doorway. I smiled and said, "Louise, sit down and have a cup of coffee with me."

She looked uncertain and timidly said, "I don't want to disturb you."

"I could use the company. And I didn't have the opportunity to thank you for rescuing me from Sheriff Price. We don't seem to get along too well."

"It was nothing." Louise poured a cup of coffee and sat down next to me. "I didn't think it was proper for the sheriff to talk to you like that. He was so rude. You're helping Mr. Johnson?"

Louise, who was almost sixty years old, lived alone in a small trailer park near the beach. "Alone, but not lonely, never lonely. I've got the ocean, my shell collection, my birds, and my little garden to keep me busy." The older woman had virtually adopted Amanda, constantly called her "the daughter I never had."

"Louise, I know you're upset, but I need your help. Was Amanda having any problems? Did she seem to be upset about anything lately?"

She paused, weighing loyalty to her company against her devotion to Amanda. It didn't take long, devotion won. Her words were a soft whisper. I leaned across the table, straining to hear. "I was worried 'bout her. She wasn't eating or sleeping. Why, I'd come in early in the morning and find her hunched over that computer; she'd been working all night and was surprised to find that daylight had come around again."

"Did she do that often?" Louise shook her head no. "Did she stay late last week?" Louise signaled yes. "How many times?"

"Most every night. She was worried. I can always tell when she's worried. It always shows." Louise slipped into the present tense; I didn't correct her.

"I think she and Mr. Johnson were having some troubles. I heard them arguing. Mind you, I wasn't eavesdropping; it's just hard to ignore them when they fight. He yells and she yells right back. They had a fight on Tuesday, no, it was on Monday. It was real loud, and I don't mean maybe. I could hear them all the way out by my desk and the door was closed. Mr. Johnson came rushing out: He was in a terrible temper. I went into Mrs. Johnson's office; she was trying to hide it but I could tell, she was crying. I asked what was wrong but she pretended she didn't hear me. She just started talking about some project. She left soon after that. I never saw her again.''

"Did they have other fights?" I pushed Louise, once again taking advantage of her grief. But that's part of my job. I ignored the tears running down her face and asked again, "Did you hear other arguments?"

"Not like this one. This was different. I don't know. I can't explain—it was different. She was so upset..."

Crack. My back was to the doorway but I didn't need to turn around. Gum-chewing Jennifer sauntered into the room. She stared at Louise and said to me, "I've been looking for you." Crack. She held out a folder and said, "Here's your list." Crack.

I wanted to rip the gum from her mouth and stick it on the tip of her nose but I didn't. I wanted the file that was clutched in those carefully manicured fingers. Jennifer handed the folder across the table, cracked the gum one last time, and swayed out on three-inch heels. My calves ached in sympathy.

Louise nervously stuffed her napkin into the empty Styrofoam cup and excused herself. "I've got to go. They'll be looking for me."

BEING ON TIME is my not-so-secret obsession. I always arrive at meetings, parties, and other events early, wondering why it has happened again. I've learned to carry extra cigarettes and a book, and not to get too frustrated.

Tonight was no exception. I hurried into the Caribbean Room five minutes early, late by my standards. I fought through plastic palm trees to the bar and claimed a stool far away from the golfers dressed in clashing pink, green, yellow, and blue clothing, replaying the afternoon's round in voices almost as loud as their clothing.

The bartender, earnestly tan and friendly, slapped a coaster on the bar and waited. The rows of gleaming bottles, the wooden handles of the beer taps, the sparkling glasses, the olives, tempted me. I took a deep breath, and said, "Seltzer. Hold the lime."

I ordered a second, then a third glass of seltzer and looked at my watch. I had been stood up. One of the golfers noticed my plight and offered to act as stand-in for my absent date; dinner with a man dressed in green plaid pants and a red sweater was not an appetizing thought. I'd rather eat a solitary room service dinner.

I stalked out to the lobby and punched the elevator button with more force than necessary. The doors slid open and I had one foot inside the elevator when Hugh called my name. He caught my arm and said, "Blaine, didn't you receive my message? I got hung up at the hospital. Someone was supposed to call, tell you I'd be late. I hope you didn't think I wasn't going to show up." He smiled. "I spent the whole day waiting for it to be time to see you again."

My annoyance vanished with his smile. In the two and a half years since Jeff died, I'd attempted a few casual, disastrous dates. Those evenings always ended up with me home early, alone and feeling guilty. Finally, I gave up and refused all invitations. It was easier to stay home and drink myself to sleep. "Give it time" was the advice I used to console myself. "Give it time." Hugh's smile flashed again. I checked, couldn't find any guilt, and returned his smile.

We walked through the bar to the dining room. The room was quiet; the golfers had disappeared. A table overlooking the marina was waiting. Dinner passed quickly, accompanied by Hugh's lighthearted conversation.

Coffee arrived. Hugh suggested a drink instead of dessert and attempted to steer the conversation to more serious matters. I'm overly sensitive to questions by strangers and don't have any desire to provide amusing stories for their next cocktail party. I interrupted his question about my work. "Please, it's been such a pleasant evening. Let's not ruin it by talking about business." I pressed my face against the window and said, "It's not raining. Instead of an after-dinner drink, how about an after-dinner walk on the beach?"

We went out to the beach. Hugh paused at the bottom of the walkway leading to the beach, slipped off his shoes, and dropped them to the sand under the boardwalk. "We can leave our shoes here. Don't worry, no one will steal them—it's not like New York City."

I let the slur on my hometown pass without comment. It's been a long time since I was provoked into arguing about subways, crime, or overcrowding. Let those people stay away; I don't feel any urge to enlighten them. I smiled and added my sandals to the small pile.

We strolled along the edge of the water, dodging waves and lightly holding hands. Hugh pointed to a distant lighthouse. "That old lighthouse has stood there for almost one hundred fifteen years. Six of them were built to protect ships coming up the coast. This one is special because it's the only one that marks a harbor entrance; it's also the only one that still works." The beam swept through the dark sky, confirming his words. "The old bearded light keeper is gone. The entire system was automated about ten years ago. Each lighthouse is painted black and white, but with different patterns so sailors can tell them apart. When the Lighthouse Commission got around to painting this one, they ran out of patterns. So our lighthouse is pure white with a thin strip of black at the top and bottom.''

We turned and walked back to the spot where we had left our shoes, silently agreeing it was time to leave. I was trying to balance on one foot, wipe the sand off the other foot, and get the sandal back on when I lost my balance. Hugh reached out to steady me; his arms encircled my waist and pulled me to his chest. We kissed.

I pulled him closer. We embraced and kissed again. Suddenly, without any warning or reason, he stiffened and pushed me away. His hand darted out and flipped my jacket open. ''You've got a gun!''

''So?'' Hugh didn't recognize the warning in my voice.

''Do you know how I spent my day, why I was late for dinner? I was trying to save the life of a thirteen-year-old boy who was shot by his little brother. The little kid got tired being teased. He got his daddy's gun from the nightstand and shot his brother. The boy's probably going to die because his parents were stupid enough to keep a loaded gun in the house where a little kid could get hold of it. And you have the nerve to show up for a date with a pistol tucked under your arm.''

The venom is his voice startled me. I tried to answer. "I'm not some kid fooling around with a gun he found in his parents' bedroom. I agree, they were stupid. But I'm not; I'm licensed and well trained. I don't go around shooting people who make me mad. For me, a gun is a necessary piece of equipment. I don't like it and rarely carry it. But this is one of those times where I felt it necessary."

"You didn't even have the courtesy to tell me...."

We were speaking in low, angry whispers, but I couldn't whisper any longer. I raised my voice. "Did you expect me to tell you? Thanks for dinner and by the way, I've got a gun. The guy in the parking lot last night didn't have the courtesy to warn me. You're the person who happened to stumble across me—how do I know you're not the guy who hit me?"

I had gone too far, but it was too late to stop. "I don't know who I can trust. Do you expect me to continue my investigation without taking any steps to protect myself? You did a nice sewing job, Doctor, but I'd rather not be a patient in your emergency room again."

"But hidden in a holster under your arm?"

My breath caught in the back of my throat and I answered slowly. "When I graduated from college, I spent some time on the New York City police force. I had a partner who always carried her gun in her purse. One day I watched helplessly as Anna fumbled in her damn purse for her gun. She got killed before I could help. I swore that if I was ever again in a situation dangerous enough for me to carry a gun, that gun would be within easy reach. What happened to Anna would never happen to me." I wasn't interested in Hugh's response. I turned and ran up the wooden stairs, wiping tears from my eyes.

THREE

A COVERED STAIRCASE on the outside of the building was the quickest, and most deserted, route back to my suite. I ran up the stairs, groped in my jacket pocket for the key, and realized I was carrying only one sandal. Its mate was on the beach and would stay there until later, after Hugh was gone.

I muttered, "Silly gun," jammed the key into the lock, and stopped. The door was unlocked. My heart began to pound—that door had been securely locked earlier in the evening.

The gun was no longer silly. I yanked it from the holster, placed the sandal on the mat, and quietly pushed the door open. I slid through the narrow opening, noiselessly closed the door behind me, and waited for my eyes to adjust to the shadows, scarcely daring to breathe.

A lumpy object lay in the center of the room. I daintily stepped over it and tiptoed into the suite, my ears straining to hear the sound of an intruder's breathing, my eyes straining to detect movement in the darkness. I moved into the living room. It was empty. So was the kitchen. And the bedroom. And the bathroom.

I returned to the vestibule, turned on the bright overhead light, looked down at the lump on the floor, and gagged. A large, dead rat was stretched out on the carpet. Blood dribbled from the neck which has been almost completely severed from the body. A glazed eye stared at me. My stomach started to heave: dinner rose in my throat. I sprinted to the bathroom.

Rats, dead or alive, terrify me. Whoever planted this one couldn't have known and couldn't have picked a more effective method of trying to rattle me. Just a lucky guess that worked—I was frightened.

My hands were shaking. I grabbed a bottle of mouthwash from the counter and took an enormous mouthful, trying to wash the sour taste of vomit from my mouth, working up the nerve to go back out. I turned on the water faucet and splashed some water on my face. It didn't help. I stuck my entire head under the gushing cold water, gulped some air, and convinced myself to leave the bathroom.

The rat was dead; it couldn't hurt me. I didn't believe it, but I managed to inch closer. Blood was caked on the dark fur; a small puddle of drying blood had formed under the body, staining the beige carpet.

An envelope, its corner soaked with blood, was stuck under the carcass. My stomach started to churn. I ignored the wild rolls, swallowed hard, and used the barrel of my pistol to nudge the rat aside. I gingerly pulled the envelope free and walked into the living room, my stomach pitching and heaving with each step. I dropped the blood-spattered envelope on the desk, fished a newspaper from the garbage can, and went back to cover the dead animal.

Once the rat was hidden from sight, my hands stopped shaking. I sat behind the desk, called housekeeping to clean up the mess, lit a cigarette, and opened the envelope, studiously avoiding the wet corner. I buried the bloody envelope under some papers in the wastepaper basket and unfolded the note.

The message was simple and direct. Large, red-crayon block letters spelled out, GO HOME. QUIT MEDDLING. To underscore the point, the author circled the words with a few drops of blood and added a final warning, YOU COULD GET HURT!

I stared at the paper. A discreet tap at the door roused me. "Housekeeping, m'am." I stuffed the note into my pocket and went to the door, carefully edging around the newspaper on the floor. My hand was on the doorknob before I realized the gun was tightly clenched in my fist. I slipped the gun into its holster and opened the door.

Even though I had no memory of doing it, the door was chained. I peered through the crack; worried eyes looked back. A soft voice said, "Ma'am, my name is Jim Dalton. I'm the evening manager. The front desk told me you were having a problem."

I loosened the chain and wordlessly opened the door. Dalton led two men into the room, looked at the paper on the floor, looked at my face, and steered me into the living. "Miss Stewart, I am so sorry about this. Please accept our apologies for this and the mishap you suffered last night. We have instructed Dr. Reynolds and the hospital to send us all the bills for their services."

He gestured at the men who had removed the rat and were now busy applying carpet cleaner to the stain. "I don't understand how this happened. Would you feel more comfortable in another room? I can move you immediately."

The offer was tempting, but I wasn't going to be frightened into scurrying to another room. And if I did move, it wouldn't take the rat person long to find me—Dolphin Beach is a small town. I said, "No, thank you. There isn't any reason for me to change rooms."

Although we both knew it was a lie, I said, "This was an accident; you don't have to apologize. As for last night, the inn can't be held responsible for a mugger in the parking lot." Relief spread across the man's face, his lawsuit worries evaporated. "Don't worry; I'm not going to make a fuss. These incidents haven't been your fault. But I appreciate your concern."

The cleanup crew quietly packed their equipment and left, a wet spot on the rug all that remained. The manager followed them to the door and said, "I've been at Harbour House for twenty years now. I've seen all kinds of crazy things but this is one of the craziest. If you need anything, anything at all, you come to me. I'll take care of it myself." It felt good to have an ally.

The phone rang; it was Eileen. I marveled at her perfect timing. She has an uncanny ability to sense when things have gone wrong. Tonight was no exception.

After listening to my feeble "Hello," she demanded, "Blaine, you're upset. What's wrong?"

The sympathy in her voice melted my resolve to not be upset by the intimidation attempt. Everything flooded out in a rush. "My head has been throbbing all day. I had a fight with my dinner date because he didn't like my gun. I came back to my room—alone—and tripped over a dead rat on the floor. It was anchoring a threatening note. That's why I'm upset, and you've only heard the highlights."

Eileen ignored my hysterical outburst, which was the best way to deal with it, and quietly said, "Tell me about the note."

"There isn't much to tell. The writer suggested that I mind my own business and go home before I get hurt. Of course, the note wasn't signed. People who leave dead animals and bloodspattered threats are usually too cowardly to sign their name."

"Send the note up to me by courier. I'll have it analyzed." Eileen never gives up; she believes in exhausting all possibilities. It's a family trait, so I didn't comment on the futility of analyzing block letters, printed with a crayon on standard typing paper. Eileen asked one of her favorite questions. "How are you?"

"Well"—I took a few seconds to light a cigarette and think about her question—"you know I don't react well to threats." We both laughed. "If the jerk who did this thinks I'm going to pack up and leave town, he better think again. Someone has gone to a lot of trouble to scare me off, I must be close to something important. It's too bad I don't know what that something is. I'm going to stick it out, be persistent."

Eileen laughed again and said, "You're not persistent, you're stubborn. Just be careful, I don't like the idea of somebody being able to get into your room."

Neither did I, but I wouldn't admit it. We talked for a few more minutes and then hung up. Still enervated, I held onto the phone, needing to hear a friendly voice, a person who would understand and offer comfort. Without thinking, I pulled the telephone closer and dialed my home telephone number. The phone rang twice, the answering machine clicked, and my voice said to me, "Please leave your name, number, and a message. I'll get back to you as soon as possible."

Tears rose in my eyes. I slammed the phone down and paced around the room. No one would answer. No one was waiting for my call. I was alone.

The loneliness was unbearable; it pounded inside my chest, growing stronger and more painful with each heartbeat. I went out onto the balcony, smoked cigarette after cigarette, and stared at the white foam of the waves crashing on the beach, missing Jeff, and worrying about my life. The rain finally drove me back inside the lonely rooms.

Earlier in the day the hotel management, as part of their effort to atone for the attack in the parking lot, had sent flowers, a fruit basket, and two bottles of wine. When it arrived, I had appreciatively sniffed the flowers, eaten an apple, and ignored the wine.

I walked inside, shaking rain from my hair; the slender, dark green bottles on the table caught my eye. I wanted a drink, enough drinks to let me sleep. My body ached with the desire to uncork those bottles. I grabbed a can of seltzer from the refrigerator and drained it in two quick swallows.

The seltzer didn't help; I knew the wine would. If I opened a bottle, I wouldn't have to think or care. I would be able to sleep, undisturbed by dreams. I would also hate myself.

I'm an alcoholic. Quite an unusual one; it took me only six months to reach that stage. I started drinking after my husband was killed. I'd have a few drinks in the evening, to help me sleep—I didn't believe in sleeping pills.

The nightcaps turned into after-dinner drinks, then drinks during dinner, and then drinks while I cooked dinner. Within months, I was drinking from the minute I walked into my apartment after work until I was ready to pass out. Sometimes I managed to stumble to bed before passing out, but I usually collapsed on the sofa, got up in the morning, dragged myself to work, came home in the evening, and started drinking again.

And soon I drank continuously from Friday night to Sunday night, never leaving my apartment, rarely bothering to dress, wash my face, or even brush my teeth. No one ever suspected that my weekends consisted of drinking bottle after bottle of wine, scotch, beer, or vodka—I didn't care what I was drinking.

Six months ago, during a rare sober period, I examined my face in the mirror. The eyes were listless and hard; the drawn face was lifeless. I didn't recognize this person. I didn't want to know this person. I didn't want to be this person. I couldn't anaesthetize myself any longer.

I left that mirror, went into the kitchen, opened every bottle, and poured the contents of each one into the sink, sobbing as the liquid poured down the drain—they were my friends, my only comfort, and I was throwing them away.

These new bottles tempted me. The wine would erase the vision of Amanda's body from my mind and bring the dreamless sleep my body craved. I stood in front of the wine bottles and idly ran my fingers over the tops, thinking. It would be so easy to open a bottle, fill a glass...

I picked up a bottle, held it for a second, then grabbed both bottles and put them in the hallway—let someone else enjoy them. I weakly leaned against the door; they were too close, too available. I grabbed my slicker and ran out to the beach.

FOUR

Saturday

A DOWNPOUR rattling the windowpanes woke me. I shrugged into a bathrobe, went to the bedroom window, and pushed the curtains aside. The wind slammed horizontal sheets of rain against the glass, and waves smashed onto the beach. I craned my neck to look at the sky, found dark clouds and decided to skip my morning run. Usually I enjoy running in bad weather but this storm was too violent. This was a perfect day to stay inside.

I brewed a pot of coffee and restlessly paced around the suite, telling myself to sit and work. I couldn't put off the drudgery any longer. I sighed, retrieved my meager set of clues from their hiding places, and carried them to the desk. They made a very small pile.

Amanda's calendar, a spreadsheet, a list of employees—not much to show for two days' work. I leaned back in the chair and wondered which item had caused the attack in the parking lot, which one had prompted the rat, and which one would direct me to Amanda's killer.

The diary's inner pockets held a calendar and small notebook. Amanda's precise handwriting filled page after page of the notebook with comments on meetings, telephone conversations, and project ideas. I scanned the book and laid it aside; the calendar would be easier to decipher.

I looked through the calendar, frowned, and turned to the notes I had taken while sitting with Boyd, listening to his story of Amanda's disappearance. My memory was correct. Amanda had meetings scheduled for Tuesday. I went back to the calendar and frowned again. Nothing. No meetings Tuesday. None in Wilmington, none in her office.

One notation puzzled me. Friday's block held a single entry: "7 A.M.—Jessica." No surname, no location, no indication of the business to be discussed. I studied the employee list, address book, and notebook, searching for a mention of Jessica and didn't find any. I tossed the calendar down in frustration— maybe Jessica was the cleaning lady.

I returned to the notebook and carefully read every entry. After three cups of coffee from the second pot, I hadn't learned anything. Four more pages. I poured one last cup of coffee and resisted the urge to turn on the television; lying on the sofa, watching Saturday morning cartoons would be more productive.

Persistence pays—or so I kept reminding myself. But it didn't pay this time; I reached the end of the little book with a headache, a sour stomach, a myriad of jumbled impressions but no ideas. I idly flipped through the pages, randomly rereading entries.

My name jumped off the last page. I had somehow managed to overlook Amanda's minuscule reminder for Friday's appointment, the one we never kept. It was an ominous entry: "Blaine 10:30—Jessica/ *COCAINE*."

Persistence paid—and I didn't know what it was telling me. Except Amanda's death could no longer be attributed to senseless, random violence. My mission was simple: prove it.

The rain had slowed to a soft mist—perfect running weather—and I needed to clear my head. I stuffed the papers into my camera case, locked it, buried the case in the bottom of the bedroom closet, and changed into running clothes.

Running with a gun isn't comfortable, but I preferred life to comfort. The automatic was securely tucked under my windbreaker when I stepped outside. I had become a true believer in the old cliché of being safe, not sorry.

I skipped the stretching exercises and started with a slow jog to warm up but gave up after two or three miles. My legs muscles were tight, my lungs were burning, my motivation gone. I didn't feel like running.

I turned to walk back to the hotel and realized I didn't feel like going there either. I walked along the water, aimlessly kicking seashells into the waves. I squinted into the rain and saw the faint outline of a fishing pier. It's always good to have a goal. So I pulled the hood up over my hair and set a goal of reaching that pier. At least I could be sure of accomplishing something today.

The pier was almost deserted. Only a few dedicated fishermen, and women, were out in the bad weather.

I strolled to the end of the T-shaped boardwalk, returning the friendly nods of the people I passed, smiling at their comments about the weather and their luck, or lack of luck. It was easy to sympathize with those who weren't having any luck.

Rain and fog obscured the view. I stood at the end of the pier and watched the harbor light sweep around every ninety seconds, struggling to pierce the mist. A creepy feeling, the one that happens when someone is watching me, crawled along the back of my neck. I tried to ignore it, blaming too many cups of coffee on an empty stomach. The feeling became stronger, too strong to ignore.

I unzipped my windbreaker and casually turned to look back to the shore. A solitary fisherman was walking toward me, a fishing pole and tackle box in his left hand, his right hand nonchalantly stuck in his jacket pocket. I leaned against the railing and watched. He stopped a few feet from me, put the tackle box down on the rough boards, crouched beside it, and opened the plastic box.

The lid obscured my view of the box's contents. I watched, knowing I should move, but my feet were firmly stuck to the pier. He reached into the tackle box; my right hand simultaneously moved inside my jacket, grasped the butt of my gun, and gently eased it out of the holster.

A quick, stupid thought passed through my mind—I almost smiled. Was Eileen good enough to extricate me from the mess a shoot-out on the pier would leave?

Was I good enough to avoid becoming a mess on the pier?

The man removed hooks and a bait container from the tackle box. I laughed from nervous relief—too much coffee—let my grip on the pistol relax and instantly tightened it when he softly called my name.

"Who are you?" I took a step closer for a better look at his face.

He looked down, hiding his face from me, and said, "Doesn't matter. You smoke? Here, take one."

He held out a wrinkled pack of cigarettes. I took a cigarette and, in spite of the baseball cap pulled low over his forehead, recognized his face, "Why, you're that cop. Da—"

"Like I said, you don't need to know my name." His attention appeared to be focused on skewering a tiny fish from the bait container. "People around here are getting nervous about you and the questions you're asking." He stood up and cast the line, nodding with satisfaction when it hit the water.

"If this is a threat, forget it. I'm sick of threats. Tell whoever sent you it won't work." I flicked cigarette ash into the water and said, "I don't scare easily. And I'm not leaving Dolphin Beach until I'm ready."

"I'm not trying to scare you. But you should be careful; people are getting real nervous 'bout you."

"Who's getting nervous? And why?"

Davis avoided my gaze. "Things were going okay down here until Mrs. Johnson got killed and you started poking around. People are worried you might stir up trouble, find things that shouldn't be found."

"Now I'm really curious. I love riddles." Davis's rod bent to the water. He reeled in a few feet of line; I kept talking. "But I'm too wet, tired, cold, and hungry to play games with you. Thanks for the cigarette; I owe you one. Good luck with the fish."

He grabbed my arm. "Wait." I didn't have much choice. I waited, impatiently tapping my fingers against the railing. A few people wandered over, eager to watch him land the fish. "Too many people around here now. You fish?" I nodded and he said, "Good. I'll meet you here tomorrow morning. I'll be here by six. We'll have lots of time to talk—no interruptions."

I agreed, tossed my cigarette into the water, adding it to the litter of fast-food wrappers floating on the tide, and slowly jogged back to the hotel. My mind was occupied with thoughts of drugs, threats, rats, and traps.

I TOOK A SHOWER and paced around the suite, my mind furiously working. The sterile white walls brought out latent claustrophobic feelings. I had to get out, away from the stale, cigarette-scented air in the tiny rooms. Maybe lunch would help.

I grabbed my keys, took the Porsche from its sheltered parking space, and drove out of town. My late-afternoon search for lunch was not successful. Truck stops, barbecue joints, and fast-food outlets dominated the landscape. Hardee's dwindled to sporadic run-down restaurants and eventually gave way to fields dotted with abandoned tobacco sheds, their tin roofs browned with rust. Not a single restaurant, decent or dirty, was in sight.

I drove into a deserted intersection and let the car idle in neutral while I looked around. Left, right, or straight? Left won the mental coin toss. Ten miles and more fields, tumbledown shacks, and graying farmhouses later, I was regretting the choice and ready to admit my mistake.

Ever the optimist, I promised my rumbling stomach, "Five more minutes, then I'll turn around." I flew past a small brick farmhouse before the message on a sign in front of the house registered. The sign promised good food and drink. More importantly, it promised lunch.

"A big warm bun and a huge hunk of meat. Cheeseburger in Paradise. Medium rare with mustard be nice. Heaven on earth with an onion slice." I sang off-key, made a quick U-turn, and pulled into the gravel drive.

The cheeseburger was better than the one in the song; maybe my luck was changing. I sat, my back to the bar, and stared out the window at the rain, lost in daydreams.

A familiar voice broke into my reverie. It was Hugh, interrupting my fantasy of nude sunbathing on a deserted beach. "Blaine, I thought that was your car parked outside—there aren't too many like that around town. I was on my way home from the hospital." He looked around the room. "Are you by yourself? Do you mind if I join you?"

I motioned to the empty chair opposite me. "I'm alone, please sit." I was still angry and didn't waste the opportunity to let him know. "But I should warn you; I've got a gun."

My comment hit its target. Hugh sat down, loosened his tie, and said, "I guess I deserved that; I also owe you an apology for last night. I overreacted. But I've seen too many gunshot victims. It's so senseless.... I couldn't forget about that kid in the emergency room." He shook his head and stared at the tablecloth.

"How is he?"

Hugh looked up and said, "Danny? He died this morning."

The silence lengthened. I drained the iced tea glass and carefully put it down on the lacy tablecloth. Carefully replacing glassware was a remnant of my drinking days when knocking over a glass would call attention to the amount of alcohol I had consumed. "Hugh, I'm sorry about the boy. And I'm sorry we argued."

I wiped condensation from the glass with my index fingers and wished I hadn't left my cigarettes in the car. "It's your turn to be understanding. I tried to explain last night: Sometimes my job turns a little violent." I squirmed, unaccustomed to talking about, and defending, my work.

Hugh opened his mouth; I cut him off. "I don't enjoy carrying a gun but I do when it's necessary to save a life, especially if the life in question is mine. If someone is coming after me, or one of my clients, I don't have any choice." I paused. "I will use that gun." Hugh looked horrified. I kept my face expressionless, feeling foolish for being coerced into justifying myself. I don't often find it necessary to justify my actions.

"Have you ever—"

"Do you enjoy telling people about patients you lost?" He shook his head. "Neither do I. I refuse to be drawn into a discussion of my cases so you can have gory stories to repeat at your next cocktail party."

"Give me a little credit. I'm not looking for cocktail-party chatter. Even though you're making it difficult, I am trying to understand."

I blushed. "This isn't going to work. We're both overly sensitive about the subject. Why don't we talk about something safe, like politics, and make a solemn promise to never discuss work again?" I held out my hand. "Let's be friends again; we'll have more fun."

Hugh looked doubtful but accepted my outstretched hand. "Okay, I'll try. Now, how about dinner?"

It was almost six and most of the tables were occupied by the first wave of early dinners. Hugh's invitation was tempting but I thought of my meeting with Davis and said, "Yes, but not tonight. I have an early appointment tomorrow and I have to prepare myself."

Fortunately, Hugh didn't ask for an explanation; he wouldn't have liked the answer. We made plans to meet later in the week and I left, following the short-cut he described back to town. Except I made a short detour and parked near the fishing pier to study the layout.

Goosebumps rose on my skin. It was all wrong, too open, too exposed. I ignored the nervous fluttering of my stomach and drove back to the inn.

The evening was uneventful and boring. I spent the time performing tasks designed to keep my hands busy and my mind away from the following morning. The routine of laying out clothes, fishing gear, and extra ammunition, cleaning and loading my automatic worked. It was almost midnight when I crawled into bed for another restless night. Sleep finally arrived, accompanied by disturbing ~~dreams~~. Dreams I couldn't remember when I woke up.

FIVE

Sunday

4:00 A.M. I LAY IN BED, watching the red numbers of the digital clock flip, counting off the minutes I should have been sleeping. 4:17. I gave up the pretense of sleep and stumbled out of bed. It was time to go fishing.

Jeans, T-shirt, slicker, running shoes were waiting; I dressed quickly, automatically. Gun, holster, and elastic band for my hair completed the ensemble. I was ready.

I gathered my gear and a thermos of strong, black coffee and went out into the misty darkness. I drove to the pier, parked in the most inconspicuous spot I could find, poured some coffee, lit my first cigarette of the new week, and sat watching the sky lighten, waiting to see if anyone accompanied Davis.

5:45. Davis strolled down the street and onto the wharf, fishing pole and tackle box in hand. He walked past the four or five fishermen already on the pier, their lines cast into the water. He nodded to them and kept walking to a spot near the center of the pier. He was alone.

Davis, juggling the tackle box and other equipment, dropped a pole. A young kid, wearing a Duke baseball cap and yellow rain slicker, picked up the fishing pole and handed it to Davis.

I stubbed the cigarette out in the overflowing ash-tray, pulled away from my spot on the side street, and coasted into the lot at the pier. The unmistakable crack of a high-powered rifle sounded just as I was pushing the car door open. A second shot quickly followed the first. I ducked below the window, grabbed my pistol, and braced for another shot.

Silence. I exhaled the breath I had been holding, took a deep gulp, and cautiously peered through the windshield.

A small crowd was gathering in the center of the pier. I didn't even think about joining them. There wasn't any reason for me to walk out in the rain—I knew they were looking at Davis.

An engine roared in the quiet air. A battered pickup truck, its finish worn by the salt air to a dull gray, sped from behind a building on the corner and turned left on Harbour Drive.

My tires squealed as I backed out of the parking lot, confident the Porshce wouldn't have any trouble catching the truck. Zero to sixty in 6.1 seconds is what the advertisements promise—they don't lie. I sped through the red light at the end of the block and nar-rowed the gap between the two vehicles, close enough to read the truck's license plate, if it hadn't been smeared with mud.

The truck zigzagged down the street. I pulled closer, considered a maneuver to force the other driver to the curb, and reconsidered when I caught a glimpse of a rifle in the passenger's hands. Following at a prudent distance was good enough for the moment.

The steering wheel vibrated from slight bumps in the pavement. The car drifted to the right; I wrestled it back to the center of the road, annoyed by the sloppy handling. I felt several more thumps; the Porsche veered sharply to the right. The steering wheel shook violently beneath my hands. I slipped the transmission into neutral and coasted to the curb, my anger rising with each *whap, whap* from the rapidly flattening tire. I pounded the steering wheel with frustration and combined obscenities to form new and unique phrases. The pickup truck vanished around a bend in the road.

I climbed out of the car, muttering, cursing against tire manufacturers, defective products, sloppy workers, and their mothers. I ran out of English words, attempted a few foreign phrases, and sat on the curb, casting evil glances at the flat tire.

Tires, especially the expensive ones I purchased, don't go flat after two thousand miles. A faint hissing caught my attention: a second tire was slowly deflating. A brand new flood of curses streamed out of my mouth. I watched the second, then a third, tire go flat.

It didn't take great detective skills to find the cause. Several dozen caltrops, steel jacks with hollow spikes that can puncture the tires of any vehicle passing over them, were scattered across the pavement. I plucked one from the asphalt and gingerly bounced it in my palm; the vicious razor-sharp spikes were capable of topping the most determined pursuer.

I kicked the steel jacks into the gutter, safely away from innocent drivers on their way to Sunday church services, and redirected my curses to the driver of the pickup truck. After being sure the car doors were securely locked—I didn't want to lose my tape player too—I jogged back to the pier, not anxious to return to the scene.

It was too late for anyone to help Davis. The parmedics paused to pronounce him dead and cover the body before turning to the other person lying on the rough, wooden planks. For once, I wanted a clear view. I pushed and shoved through the crowd until I was inside the tight ring of onlookers.

The ambulance crew feverishly worked on the kid who had bent down to pick up Davis's fishing pole. The boy was almost six feet tall and slender. His long, reddish hair hung below the collar of his blood-stained workshirt. Shot in the back.

From behind, with his baseball cap jammed on his head, his figure disguised by the loose, yellow jacket, a distant gunman could have easily mistaken the boy for my twin, if I had one—or me.

It should have been me facedown on those boards. Bitter, coffee-flavored bile rose in my throat. I whirled, pushed through the crowd, and ran into the arms of a deputy sheriff.

"Sheriff Price would like to speak with you, ma'am. He's a little busy right now. But he told me to ask you to wait for him." A small notebook appeared in his hands. "I'd like to ask you a few questions while we wait."

He asked questions, studied the answers written in the notebook, and asked the questions again. I repeated the same weary answers, taking care to face away from the circle of activity on the pier.

Finally convinced that my answers wouldn't change, the police officer stopped asking questions. He ordered me to wait for Price and left me alone with my evil thoughts. I was thoroughly shaken and dispirited, stranded in a nightmare. I lit a cigarette and stared at the troubled water.

An innocent bystander had been injured. Because he wanted to get an early start on the day's fishing. Because from a distance he looked like a tall, thin woman with long, red hair. Because I had ignored a perfectly clear warning.

Sheriff Price appeared. He leaned against the railing and growled, "What the hell are you doing here?"

I made no attempt to be civil. "I already gave my statement to your deputy."

"Well, you can give to to me again. How come you're out here?"

"This is a fishing pier; fish are in that water down there. I came out here to fish. I'm on vacation; it's not unusual for people who are on vacation to go fishing."

"Just because I talk with a Southern accent, don't mean I'm stupid. Just think for a second before you give me one of your smart-ass answers. You can answer my questions here or I can have you taken down to the station where it's quiet." He waited. When I didn't bother to answer or even look up from the water, he tried again. "You don't really expect me to believe it's coincidence that you just happened to be fishing."

I didn't think, I reacted. "I don't give a shit about what you think. Is there anything else? I'd like to get out of this rain and get some breakfast."

He replied in a low, furious voice, "Now you just listen up, lady. We are investigating a murder, a murder of one of my men. Two murders if that boy don't make it. When I ask you a question, you better answer without any big-city, smart-mouthed private investigator talk. Either you answer my questions or I'll have you handcuffed and tossed into jail until you decide to cooperate. You understand?" He interpreted my silence as agreement. "Good. I'm glad we understand each other. Now, why did you come out here this morning?"

It was too late for me to change my story. I said, "Fishing."

"Miz Stewart, I'm losing what little patience I have left. You're a stranger here, people 'round here notice strangers, especially pretty, redheaded strangers. Yesterday, a few of those people noticed you and Davis standing at the end of this pier talking. What were you two talking about? And Miz Stewart, before you answer, think for a second 'bout what it means to be charged with obstruction of an official investigation."

"Am I being charged? If so, read me my rights. I'm not saying another word until my attorney gets here." Having said that, I defiantly stared at the sheriff.

He returned the stare and said, "No, you're not being charged—not yet. If that's your story, be sure you stick to it. Let me give you a little friendly advice. Get the hell out of this goddamn town before I find a good reason to throw your ass in jail."

I flicked my cigarette over the railing and watched it spin into the water. "Sheriff, I think you're a little mixed up. Aren't you supposed to say, 'Don't leave town'? I'm not leaving. You know where I'm staying if you decide to throw my ass in jail." I whirled away from him and stomped down the long pier to find a phone so I could call a tow truck to rescue my poor crippled Porsche.

After I made the call, I walked back to the car and sat on the curb. I cradled my head in my hands and stared at my wet sneakers, barely noticing the rain or the stares of passersby. The tow truck arrived, interrupting my funk; the driver hooked up my car, promised to replace the tires, and deliver it to the inn before nightfall. He also offered a ride to the hotel. I declined and trudged back to Harbour House, not in any hurry to get there and be alone with my thoughts.

A few months ago, the morning's events would have provided an excellent reason for me to spend the remainder of the day drinking myself into a stupor. But not today. Coffee and cigarettes wouldn't help: I needed to move, to sweat the overwhelming guilt out of my system. I decided to try another long, hard run on the beach.

A steady, soaking rain was falling on the empty beach. But the rain didn't bother me—I love running in foul weather. Rain, snow, cold, I don't care. For me, the exhilaration of running is magnified by the illusion of overcoming the elements, thumbing my nose at Mother Nature. Ten fast miles passed, and I returned to the hotel feeling more courageous, even a little noble. Things would work out.

THE RED MESSAGE LIGHT on the telephone was blinking. Expecting the call to be from Hugh or Eileen, I eagerly called the front desk and was taken aback by the clerk's message. "Sheriff Price called 'bout an hour ago. He said you should call him immediately. He said to tell you it was important." The clerk, clearly impressed with the message, painstakingly called out the number and asked me to repeat it to him.

I punched out the number, my hard-won confidence evaporating with each tone. Price didn't waste any time talking about the weather. "I want you to come down to the station in the morning."

"Alone, or with an attorney?"

"You don't need to bring a lawyer to hold your hand. Now, I'm not happy you decided to ignore my advice 'bout leaving. So I reckon I should help you with your investigation. You wanted to see our reports on Mrs. Johnson. They're ready. You can also sign the statement you gave my man this morning, and I need to ask you another question or two. Now, I guess you will be going to the funeral in the morning. So, how 'bout we meet early, around seven-thirty, so you can get to the church?"

Trouble. Trouble. Trouble. Price's invitation was too casual, too friendly. Suddenly aware of the lengthy silence, I quickly agreed and got out of the conversation. The trouble sign continued to flash.

It was early, but not too early to disturb Eileen's weekend. Don, Eileen's husband, answered the call. After we exchanged brief, fond insults, he called to Eileen, "It's Blaine. Better take it in the den—sounds like business."

Eileen was laughing when she picked up the receiver. "This is an unexpected pleasure. What's up, you in some kind of trouble?"

"Not yet."

She laughed again. "Wow! This is unusual; you generally call after you're in trouble."

"Quit snickering. Would you find it more amusing if I waited until something goes wrong? I called because I wanted to hear a voice that doesn't have a Southern accent and to get some advice."

All the amusement was gone from Eileen's voice. She asked, "Do you want advice from your sister, or your attorney?"

"I'm not sure..."

"Wait a second. Let me find a pad. Don's been in here cleaning—I can't find anything." Papers rustled in the background, I heard a drawer snap closed, and Eileen came back on the line. "Okay, I found one. Go ahead. What's the problem?"

I took a deep breath and told my story. Eileen made sporadic interruptions to ask questions. The tearing sound of a page being torn from a pad came over the wire. I paused to light a cigarette; Eileen took advantage of the break to ask quietly, "Why am I getting nervous?"

The grave pitch of her voice made me uneasy. I thought, "Wait until she hears the rest," and told her of my impending meeting with Price, ending with the part that worried me, the part that had prompted my call. "We also had a brief discussion about obstruction of justice. He thinks I'm hiding something."

"He's right. Dammit, Blaine, you took law courses. Did your professors ever mention how serious the courts can be about obstruction? You're supposed to be investigating Amanda's murder, not hindering the local authorities."

"Don't lecture. Price is going to do enough of that tomorrow. Besides"—I laughed nervously—"I have a very good attorney." Eileen didn't answer. "Don't I?"

"I don't find this amusing. If the sheriff decides to charge you with obstruction, you are going to be in serious trouble. And don't count on me to come flying to your rescue. You want my advice, here it is: Cooperate." When I didn't answer, she sighed. "Honestly, I don't know why you even bothered to call me. You ask for advice, knowing you're going to ignore it. You're so—"

The argument took a familiar turn. I blurted out, "—Don't call me pigheaded!" We laughed; some, not all, of the tension disappeared. "I promise to do my best to stay out of trouble and let Justice proceed unobstructed."

The remainder of our converstion was quiet. Eileen asked more questions; I skirted around the complete answers and tried to get off the line without telling her any details of my late night visit to Amanda's office.

We finally hung up. I was exhausted. I closed my eyes and rested my head on top of the desk, trying to visualize Eileen's reaction to the diary I had hidden away.

Four hours later, I woke up. The room was dark, my neck was stiff, and a paper clip was stuck to my cheek. Half-awake, I realized that a lonely Sunday evening stretched out before me; the prospect of being cooped up in a hotel room was thoroughly depressing. Instead of trying to wake up and face the loneliness, I decided to go to bed.

I spent a restive night, tossing and turning, pursued by rats, angry men in uniforms, and children with evil grins who threw little plastic bags, filled with white powder, at me. Shortly before dawn, I gave up and took another run on the beach, exorcising the demons, and watching the sun rise over Dolphin Beach.

SIX

Monday

MONDAY MORNING'S sunshine didn't last long; tropical storm Hannah made a U-turn and blew back to land, dumping a hard rain over the town. I left for the police station dressed in a black silk suit, incongruously topped with a yellow rain slicker.

Ned, the tow truck operator, had kept his promise—the Porsche was in the lot. The valet produced the keys, the observation that all the tires were as good as new, and the charge receipt. I stuck the receipt in the glove box; maybe it could pass Eileen's eye as a business expense.

THE AUTOPSY REPORT was brief and grisly. Amanda had been beaten and shot, dumped in the marsh, and left to bleed to death. Medical attention might have saved her life. My eyes misted; I blinked rapidly and scanned the other reports.

The summary of the police investigation was as sparse as the preceding report. No suspects. The car, a high-priced foreign sports model, was still missing. No sign of her wallet or purse. No sign of rape. Probably a bungled robbery attempt. "Husband questioned, alibi established, not considered a suspect at this time."

Price leaned back in his chair and sent smoke rings from his cigar to the ceiling as I read. I looked up from the page and said, ''This ends with a pretty emphatic statement absolving Boyd.''

He looked at the cigar ash, flicked it into the waste-paper basket, and blew another ring. I lit a cigarette to counteract the noxious fumes. Price said, ''Of course when you consider the size of the insurance, the husband looks like a prime suspect. We've gone over everything pretty carefully and are convinced he didn't kill her. We're still trying to locate her car. Once we do, I'm convinced we'll find the person who stole it and killed her. You know that type of foreign car can be worth a lot of money, especially if it's shipped to South America or chopped up for parts. I think she picked up a hitchhiker and got killed when he tried to rob her.''

The cigar was burning to Price's satisfaction. He grunted, tapped it on the rim of the garbage pail, and said, ''Now before it gets too late, I'd like to ask you a few questions about yesterday.'' He pulled a tape recorder from a drawer, set it on the desk between us, and slipped a cassette into it. ''I'd kinda like to have an official record of our little talk.'' He smiled. ''Hope you don't mind.''

Of course I minded but there was no room for objection. I returned his smile, waited, and thought about the advice Eileen had once given me about depositions. ''Just say 'yes,' 'no,' or 'I don't recall.' The people who talk too much are the ones who get into trouble.''

Price pushed the record button down and asked the standard opening questions of name, address, and occupation. The cigar went out, he paused to relight it, then asked, "When did you first meet Officer Davis?"

"Thursday evening."

"Where did you meet him?"

"At the Johnson residence. He escorted us, Mr. Johnson and myself, to the site where Mrs. Johnson's body was discovered."

"You'd never met Officer Davis prior to Thursday evening?"

"No."

"Was that your only contact with Davis?"

"No." I lit another cigarette.

"Describe your next meeting."

"I'm staying at the Harbour House Inn. I was mugged in the parking lot later that evening. Davis responded to the call."

"Did you make that call, requesting Officer Davis?"

"Don't you have all this in a report somewhere?" I was getting edgy, not sure where he was trying to lead me.

"Just answer the question. Who made the call?"

"I don't know; I was unconscious. Davis was there when I regained consciousness. He followed me to the hospital, asked me a lot of questions, and drove me back to the hotel."

Price smiled. Shit—I'd said too much. He asked, "What did you and Officer Davis talk about during the ride back to your hotel?"

I'd learned my lesson. I said, "Nothing," and didn't make any attempt to elaborate. Price raised an eyebrow and frowned. I decided to elaborate. "We didn't talk; I fell asleep in the patrol car. Davis had to wake me up when we reached the inn. He escorted me to my suite. I said, 'Thank you.' He said, 'You're welcome. Try to get some sleep.' I said, 'Good night.' He left. I went to bed."

The sheriff picked up a file from the desk and studied its contents. I took advantage of the brief respite to light another cigarette; the last one had sat in the ashtray and burned out.

Price leaned back and casually said, "Miz Stewart, I'm a little confused. The report Officer Davis filed states the mugging incident occurred at approximately one forty-five, Friday morning. Is that correct?"

My stomach contracted; the incandescent trouble sign flashed. I took a deep drag on the cigarette and slowly exhaled. "I don't understand. How is this related to Davis?"

"You don't have to understand. Just answer the question."

"I'm not sure. I didn't look at my watch but that sounds right."

A tight, satisfied grin appeared on Price's face. I forced myself to look unconcerned. He looked back into the file and read, "After leaving the site where

Mrs. Johnson's body was discovered, you drove Mr. Johnson back to their residence at 719 Bayview Avenue. Is that correct?''

"Yes."

Price went back to the file, and I took a lung-filling drag on the cigarette, praying the nicotine would have a steadying influence. The direction of Price's questions was clear to me now.

"Mr. Johnson has stated you left his residence at approximately eleven-forty Thursday evening. The Harbour House Inn is a ten or fifteen minute drive from his house. Mr. Johnson has also stated that you attempted to badger him into allowing you to search his late wife's office that evening. He says you were quite disappointed when he refused. Miz Stewart did you spend the two hours it took you to arrive at your hotel searching Mrs. Johnson's office?''

I got to my feet. "That's it. I have been trying to cooperate, but this is ridiculous. I'm not answering any more of these questions."

Price was not concerned. He waved his cigar in the air and said, "Sit down, Miz Stewart, we are not finished. Please answer the question."

"I think I should call an attorney."

Price stood up and held out a placating hand. "Hold on now, you don't need any attorney. We're not charging you with anything. Here now, sit down and catch your breath. Let me get you a cup of coffee."

I almost refused, afraid my hands would shake too much, but I reconsidered; maybe he should see my shaking hands. The sheriff poured a stale cup of coffee and put it in front of me. I pulled another cigarette from the pack; after two unsuccessful attempts, I managed to light it. Price watched without comment. Reminding myself to be careful, I stared at the burning cigarette, took a deep, audible breath, and started to answer. "No, I didn't go directly to the hotel." Price leaned forward, scrutinizing my face. "You see, I was very upset. Amanda and I were friends; we attended college together. Seeing her body was shocking—"

"Come on, who are you trying to fool? You're in the business. Surely you've seen dead bodies before."

I looked into his eyes and snapped, "Yes, but they haven't been the bodies of friends." My anger impressed him; he nodded and leaned back.

"Driving always helps me relax; it's a great way to get away from everything. That's exactly what I did Friday night after I left Boyd. I drove around, smoking cigarettes, and listening to the radio. After a while, and it could have been an hour and a half, I stopped at an all-night Piggly Wiggly to get some groceries and drove back to the inn. Someone jumped me in the parking lot. You know the rest; it's in your report."

"Did anyone see you?"

"I may have passed a few cars on the road. The supermarket was the only stop I made." Not a very good alibi, but it was the best I could do on such short notice.

Price's demeanor wasn't casual; he leaned forward and said, "You didn't go anywhere near BAJ Enterprises."

I steadily returned his gaze. "No. I had already made arrangements with Boyd to go there the following morning." I looked at my watch. "Are we almost finished? I don't want to be late."

"You'll have plenty of time to get to the church; I only have a few more things to ask. Tell me about your meeting with Davis on Saturday."

"What meeting? I went for a walk on the pier. Davis came along to fish; he recognized me and said hello. We talked about fishing. I like to fish and decided to try my luck Sunday morning. Davis said he'd look for me. I was parking my car when he was shot."

The sheriff asked more questions, jumping back and forth from topic to topic, trying to lull me into complacent carelessness. It didn't work; I had conducted too many similar interviews to be fooled by his tactics. He was good; without any change in expression, he finally slipped the question he had been working up to into the conversation. "Did you and Officer Davis ever discuss cocaine?"

"Cocaine?" I shook my head. "We talked about fishing. Was Davis involved with drugs?"

Worry lines creased his forehead. Price slowly answered. "We found a large quantity of cocaine among his personal effects. It appears that Officer Davis was heavily involved with Dolphin Beach's drug dealers. The shooting was probably related. Of course, we don't have any solid leads yet, but we're working round the clock on it. Nobody gets away with killing one of my men.''

Our conversation was veering back to dangerous territory, I interrupted. ''Sheriff, how's the boy who was shot?''

''He'll be fine; the wound wasn't as serious as it looked.'' Price noticed my surreptitious glance at the clock. He shut off the tape recorder and said, ''That's enough for today; I know you're anxious to get to the church.'' He mumbled, ''Thank you for your co-operation,'' and dismissed me.

It was 9:00 A.M., half an hour before the funeral service was to begin. Enough time to have a cup of coffee and to make the progress report Eileen was waiting to hear. I found a small restaurant and took a cardboard container of lukewarm coffee to the phone booth near the rest rooms.

Our receptionist, Marcella, was glad to hear my voice; her friendly greeting sent a wave of homesickness washing over me. Marcella is my ally; she keeps me well informed about the important gossip and rumors floating around the office. More importantly, Marcella always warns me in a voice faintly tinged with a French accent whenever Eileen is in a foul mood. Her usual phrase, ''Your sister, she is not happy this morning,'' was enough warning. I would grab a mug of coffee and creep into my office; it's easier to deal with Eileen after a large cup of strong, black coffee. Today Marcella was not encouraging. She whispered, ''Eileen has been waiting for your call.

I must warn you, her mood is very bad this morning.''

Very bad was an understatement. Eileen didn't waste time saying "Hello" or "How are you?" She asked, "What happened?" and listened without interruption—very unusual behavior—as neither one of us can listen to a story without question or comment.

I hurried my summary, puzzled by her silence, and ended with a lame, "That's it."

Eileen's reply was unexpected. She said, "Stan Adams from CIG called this morning. We had a long, uncomfortable conversation; he wanted a progress report on your investigation. Boyd's attorneys are pressing CIG for a settlement; they accused CIG of dragging its corporate feet. Evidently, from what you just told me, the police agree. There isn't any reason for CIG to delay settling the claim.''

"Uh-huh." I couldn't think of anything else to say.

"I was hoping for a response a little more articulate than 'uh-huh.' It's difficult to defend you when I'm having my own serious doubts. Stan is concerned—so am I. Blaine, is it possible you're overreacting, seeing a conspiracy that doesn't exist? You've told me a hundred times that professionals must remain objective. Maybe you've lost your objectivity, or never even had it. You were right the other night: We shouldn't work for friends. I'm worried. Tell me you haven't gone off on a wild tangent, chasing bad guys that don't exist."

My first impulse was to slam the phone down and stalk away from everything. I fought it and tried to keep my voice under control. "We took the job and I'm doing the job. Tell Adams to back off and leave me alone. I'm trying to save his shareholders some money. Dammit, it's only been four days since Amanda was killed. Why is he in such a fucking hurry to give away five and a half million dollars?"

"Stan wants a final report by Thursday."

Eileen's voice was devoid of expression; mine wasn't. I shouted, "Thursday!" The people at the counter looked up from their eggs; every head swiveled in my direction. I waited until they lost interest and turned back to their breakfast specials. "Today's Monday, I'm going to lose the entire day because of the funeral. I know Amanda wasn't killed by an inept robber. I can feel it. You've got to call Adams and convince him to extend the deadline."

"Let me be sure I understand. You want me to call CIG, tell them you have a bad feeling, and could we please have some more time?"

"Yeah, but could you make it sound more lawyerlike? Stan loves to hear you talk legal."

My feeble attempt at humor didn't work. Eileen was not happy. "I'm not laughing. Adams said Thursday. He wouldn't listen to me; he's certainly not going to be swayed by your drivel."

"Drivel!" The heads at the counter turned; I ignored them. "If you won't do it, I'll call myself—"

"Don't waste your quarter. He doesn't want to speak to you." Click.

Amazing. I stared at the receiver; Eileen had hung up on me. I almost called back; I started to dial the number but stopped. Calling back would only intensify the argument. Anyway, I knew Eileen. She might scream and yell and even hang up on me but she would call Adams. He would agree to extending the deadline. I could count on Eileen.

9:18. Twelve minutes to the funeral. I rushed out to the car.

SEVEN

I HURRIED INTO THE cathedral and looked for an empty seat; the church was packed. An elderly man in the last pew noticed me standing in the vestibule and moved to his right, leaving the end seat free. Minutes after I settled down on the wooden bench, a young priest dressed in purple vestments walked down the nave and waited at the doorway.

My seat provided me with an unobstructed—and unwelcome—view. Two young altar boys draped a white pall over the copper coffin. The priest sprinkled holy water over the casket and began his prayer. "I bless the body of Amanda Johnson..." After the short prayer, the priest led a solemn procession to the front of the church. The coffin was wheeled to the foot of the ivory altar; lighted candles were placed around the bier. The priest paused to lay a simple wooden cross on top of the casket before mounting the altar steps.

The Mass began. I followed the cues of the other mourners, standing, kneeling, and soundlessly mouthing the responses printed in the little booklet the church provided. We sat for a reading. I forced myself to listen; maybe a passage from the Book of Wisdom would provide a little understanding.

"The just man, though he die early, shall be at rest. For the age that is honorable comes not with the passing of time, nor can it be measured in terms of years. Rather, understanding is the hoary crown for men, and an unsullied life, the attainment of old age. He who pleased God was loved; he who lived among sinners was transported. Snatched away, lest wickedness pervert his mind or deceit beguile his soul; for the witchery of paltry things obscures what is right and the whirl of desire transforms the innocent mind. Having become perfect in a short while, he reached the fullness of a long career; for his soul was pleasing to the Lord, therefore he sped him out of the midst of wickedness. But the people saw and did not understand..."

Tears trickled down my cheeks. I didn't realize I was crying until the man next to me gently patted my arm and passed me a tissue.

Time to stop listening. I blew my nose and occupied my mind by developing a to-do list: interview employees, follow up on the drug connection, talk with the accountant.... A change in the rhythm of the service brought me back to the church. The end of the service was approaching; people were stirring expectantly.

The priest circled the coffin, sprinkled holy water and incense, and said, "We reverently bring the body of our sister, Amanda Johnson, to be buried in its human imperfection...." He closed the ritual book, removed the cross from the casket, and silently watched the pallbearers move the coffin to the waiting hearse.

We all followed quietly; no one, not even the children present, broke the silence.

The funeral procession wound through town, slowly journeying to the cemetery. The trip took twenty minutes; I spent the time chain-smoking and blasting a tape from the jumbled collection of cassettes stashed under the seat.

We arrived at the cemetery and were greeted by a downpour. I battled with the slicker and finally managed to pull it out. After ruefully looking at my heels—too bad I didn't have an old pair of running shoes with me—I climbed out of the car.

The reddish-brown coffin stood alone in the rain, mourners crowded under a green canopy, trying to escape the rain; bad luck placed me directly in front of the casket. Every time I looked away, the copper magnet drew my eyes back. The priest was praying, "Give our sister Amanda peaceful rest in this grave. We commit her body to the earth from which it was made...."

Nightmarish memories of another graveyard scene overwhelmed me. Two and a half years ago, it had been my husband in that coffin. I was the grieving spouse huddled under the canopy, watching a coffin being gently lowered into an open grave. Tears flowed from my eyes; I groped in my pocket and found a damp, crumpled tissue.

I made it through the service, just as I had two and a half years ago. People brushed past, rousing me from the daymare. I cautiously navigated the muddy path to the car, shivering from the dampness and the memories. My car was trapped near the end of the line, and I turned the heater to high and waited for the traffic jam to ease. After what seemed to be an hour-long delay, we began to move. I drew a shaky breath and considered skipping the post-ceremony reception but professional curiosity overcame the need for solitude. I joined the final cavalcade to Amanda's house.

SMALL GROUPS of people were clustered in various rooms of the house, quietly talking. Occasionally a burst of laughter rang out and was quickly muffled. A large group of mourners had gathered in the dining room and were eagerly attacking the buffet laid out on the long oak table; judging from the huge piles of food being heaped on the plates, a ravenous appetite was one of grief's common side effects.

Slightly nauseated by the sight of food, I choked down a glass of seltzer and wandered into the other rooms, eavesdropping on conversations until a frosty glare from one of the participants forced me to move to the next group. Forty-five minutes later I had been through the entire house and heard a lot of what the crowd seemed to consider fascinating gossip about families, fishing, work, and local politics.

I completed the circle and returned to the dining room, frustrated and thirsty, and found myself surrounded by the same hungry people. A portly gentleman, annoyed to find his path to the food blocked, rudely tried to elbow past. I returned his glower and held my ground, childishly refusing to move. I felt better.

The seltzer bottles on the sideboard were empty. I wandered into the kitchen, hoping to find another bottle. Two women stood near the sink, their heated discussion ending abruptly when I entered. Neither bothered to acknowledge my greeting, although both knew me.

"Excuse me," I said, "I'm looking for seltzer." My apology didn't work; both women glared at me. But that didn't bother me. I was used to having people dislike me—another occupational hazard. I ignored them, opened the refrigerator, and patiently searched behind the bottles and jars.

Jennifer flashed a vicious glare at Louise and flounced out of the room. Louise turned to the sink and began to wash some of the glasses carelessly stacked on the counter.

"I'm sorry." Louise didn't respond. I raised my voice so she could hear me over the rushing water. "I didn't mean to interrupt—"

"Excuse me." She twisted the faucet off and vigorously dried her hands on a dish towel. "I must get back outside. Mr. Johnson may need my help."

"Louise"—I touched her arm lightly—"is something wrong?"

"Please," she swatted my hand away from her arm and said, "I can't stay in here..." The unspoken words, "with you" hovered in the air. Panic lit her eyes; she ran out.

I watched the door swing closed and shrugged. I had finally perfected my knack for alienating people by simply walking into a room. "I don't know..."

"Don't know what?" A soft voice interrupted my mumbling. Boyd, his silver hair sharply contrasting with his somber black suit, stood in the doorway.

"Seltzer—I can't find your secret hiding place."

He opened a cabinet above the refrigerator. "It's not such a secret place; you would have found it eventually." Boyd pulled two bottles from the cabinet. "It's been a tough morning—I need something stronger." He waved a bottle of scotch before me. "How about you?"

I lied and said, "No thanks. Seltzer will be fine." I really wanted the scotch.

Boyd took two glasses from another cabinet, filled one with ice and seltzer; the other received a generous dollop of scotch. He took a sip of the amber liquid as I watched enviously. Boyd swirled the liquid, watched the alcohol trail down the side of the glass, and without looking up at me, said, "Blaine, I want to apologize for yelling at you yesterday." His voice broke. "I couldn't sleep last night; your question about Amanda's enemies kept running through my head." He hesitated, drained the glass, and said, "Perry King kept coming to mind. He hated Amanda."

"Perry King? I haven't heard that name before. Who is he? Why did he hate Amanda?"

"A few years ago, Amanda was doing some work for a local bank. She got bored and started to play around, trying to get into other systems. She stumbled onto a program King had set up for himself. He was skimming pennies from the interest payments the bank was paying its depositors and dropping them into his dummy account. No one ever noticed that one or two cents were missing from their interest payments. Over the years, it added up to a large sum of money." Boyd refilled his glass before continuing. "The bank decided to make an example of King: They prosecuted and won. During the trial he made a lot of wild threats but Amanda never took them seriously. He was recently released from jail; maybe Amanda should have paid attention to those threats."

Jennifer rushed in and called out, "Boyd, honey—" She realized I was still in the room and quickly assumed a businesslike tone. "Father Preston and other people are leaving. They're looking for you."

I followed Boyd into the living room and watched from a secluded corner. He was immediately surrounded by well-wishers. Jennifer acted as hostess, floating in the background directing the flow of traffic. People who lingered too long had their condolences cut off and were smoothly ushered to the door; another group quickly replaced them. After watching for a few minutes, I set my glass down on the mantel and went off in search of a bathroom.

The crowd was still gathered in the dining room, picking at the remains of the buffet. I pushed through them to the staircase and went up; my infallible intuition warned me that the bathrooms on the ground floor would be occupied.

So were the bathrooms on the second floor. I sat on a bed and lit a cigarette to occupy my waiting time.

Eternity is waiting for an empty bathroom after drinking a liter of seltzer.

A short woman, her close-cropped black hair high-lighted with gray streaks, came out and attempted to start a conversation. However, I was not in any condition to start a polite conversation. I hurried into the bathroom.

The woman was still waiting when I came out, rigidly perched on the edge of the bed. A cool, appraising glance swept over me. I self-consciously straightened my jacket and returned the appraisal. Fifty, maybe fifty-five, years old. Gold wire-rimmed glasses, the type popular twenty years ago, magnified serious, brown eyes.

Her silent test ended, I received a passing grade—met whatever invisible standards she was judging me against. She asked, "Are you Blaine Stewart?" I nodded. "Forgive me for being impolite." She extended a business card and said, "I conduct a legal practice in town. Would it possible for you to meet with me today? It is imperative that we talk."

The card was simple. KATHERINE H. LOURDES, ESQ. and an address were embossed on its surface. I popped the card with my index finger and said, "Sounds important. We seem to be alone now. Let's talk."

"I would prefer to meet in my office." Anger flashed in the brown eyes. "I can assure you I am not going to waste your time. It is common knowledge in Dolphin Beach that you are investigating Amanda Johnson's murder. I believe I have some information you will find useful."

Her eyes convinced me. Thankful to find a valid excuse to leave the morbid household, I agreed to the meeting and followed Lourdes down the wide staircase. Boyd was encircled by well-wishers; I pushed my way to the center and awkwardly stammered my sympathies. Boyd squeezed my hand, then turned to another caller. I backed out of the circle and walked out.

Lourdes had briskly marched past Boyd without looking in his direction. She waited for me at the edge of the driveway, impatiently kicking at the damp grass edging the driveway.

Her sensible green Pontiac led the way. It wasn't hard to keep it in sight; the speedometer never wavered above the legal speed limit. I wondered what she thought about my crimson Porsche. I was willing to bet Katherine H. Lourdes had never indulged in a flashy or impetuous act in her life. Steady, reliable, sensible: I was developing a long list of adjectives when she interrupted the process by pulling into the drive of an old—what else?—Victorian. I parked behind her.

She made the comment, "Home and office," as she unlocked the double pine doors. "I don't really like the house, but my grandfather built it over a hundred years ago. I feel obligated to keep it in the family. When my parents died, I renovated the downstairs and made it into my office. I live in the upstairs apartment." A brief smile softened her angular features. "Cuts down on the commuting. When I die, I'm leaving the house to a local historical society so it won't be torn down to make way for condominiums.

I'm not going to be the family member who sells the old homestead for a pretty piece of change. Developers have offered a lot of money for this property. I've been tempted: it would be more than enough for me to stop working and retire to the little inn on Cape Cod I've always dreamed of owning. But sometimes a person has to take a deep breath and say, 'I'm not going to sell out; the money isn't worth the price my soul would have to pay.'" The shy smile appeared again, and she said, "You are good! I don't usually talk this much to anyone, let alone strangers. You are a very good listener; that must be very useful in your occupation."

I smiled. "It helps. People tell me the strangest things. I've decided it's because of my red hair. I look like an all-American girl from the Midwest—everyone's neighbor."

Lourdes led me into her inner office. It was furnished with good ole boy furniture: leather chairs, native pine bookcases, and a handmade mahogany desk. We quickly settled into the old chairs. Lourdes, mindful of her promise not to waste my time, opened the interview by saying, "I must tell you I ran a quick check on you and your firm. I've been told you can be difficult to work with, but you have a very good reputation. Your references speak very highly of you."

"Thanks." Maybe she'd mention that to my irate sister. "But why go through all that trouble?"

She ignored my question. "The information I received about your firm consistently mentioned high ethical standards." I smiled; maybe she would repeat this to Eileen. "So I have to assume your primary interest lies in learning the truth behind Amanda's murder."

Lourdes was rolling a pencil back and forth across the desk blotter, suddenly hesitant about continuing. I leaned across the desk and put my hand over the pencil. "I'm tired of listening to people question my motives. Yes, I can be difficult to work with because I always tell people what I think. Yes, I'm working on the Johnson case. And yes, I am very interested in learning who killed her. Now if you have some information, tell me; don't play games."

"It was not my intent to question your motives." I think that was an apology. "Mrs. Johnson had scheduled an appointment with me last Tuesday evening." I wasn't surprised; the meeting had been noted in Amanda's diary. "She wanted me to represent her."

"Excuse me—the Johnsons have an attorney. Why did Amanda want to hire you?"

The tight smile reappeared. "Mrs. Johnson required her own counsel. She was planning to initiate divorce proceedings against her husband."

"A divorce?" I was startled; during the marathon talk session Amanda and I had shared six short weeks ago, a great deal of time was spent on love, relationships, and marriage. Amanda's comments were not of the type uttered by a woman contemplating divorce. Her eyes had glowed with contentment when talking about Boyd and their hopes for a family; envy had forced me to turn away. What happened?

"It was a recent decision. We had a rather lengthy telephone conversation last week. I advised her to gather various documents prior to our meeting. I also counseled her against mentioning her intentions to anyone, especially her husband. No sense in tipping him off before we were ready to proceed. It's cold-hearted advice but, as I told Mrs. Johnson, if the marriage had deteriorated to the point where she wanted to begin the termination process, she had better be prepared before delivering the news. Documents have a way of disappearing once papers are served."

Even though I had a good idea of what her answer would be, I asked, "What type of documents did you ask her to collect?"

"Nothing unusual, just standard financial information. Business and personal tax returns, financial statements, investment accounts. I'm sure you're familiar with it all. We had a prelimianry meeting scheduled for Monday evening. Mrs. Johnson canceled at the last minute. I was quite annoyed; my clients know I require twenty-four-hours' notice. Anyway, she apologized profusely and informed me she had uncovered some disturbing information. She was quite agitated and said she wanted to discuss the contents of the file with you prior to meeting with me. Mrs. Johnson and I served together as trustees for a local organization. She was not the hysterical type; that information was important." Lourdes took off her glasses, and looked deep into my eyes. "Ms. Stewart, I want to know what is in that file."

I was thinking out loud when I said, "Amanda called my office Monday afternoon. I missed her call. We never talked. Of course, I never saw her again. This is the first time a file has been mentioned to me." What did I miss in Amanda's office? "Have you told anyone else about this missing file?"

Lourdes started rolling the pencil again, troubled by my question. "No. I considered speaking to the police but decided against contacting them. All I have is speculation; I was hoping you could add something concrete." She frowned and rubbed her forehead. "I'm sorry; it seems that I have wasted your time after all."

I WASTED THE REST of the afternoon in the Dolphin Beach County Library Periodical Room. The librarian pointed to a staircase and apologized. "Newspapers are downstairs. Sorry I can't show you myself. We're shorthanded this week; it's vacation time. You just holler if you can't find what you're looking for."

The prominent No Smoking sign wasn't necessary; no sane person would dare light a match in the dirty firetrap called the Periodical Room. Simply thinking of the cigarette lighter in my purse made me nervous. Magazines and newspapers were stacked on top of bookcases and bare metal shelves; after a few minutes of searching, I deciphered the haphazard filing system and located the papers I wanted. The solitary table was littered with papers. I cleared a space and added my pile to the mess.

The embezzlement, King's arrest, subsequent trial, and parole from jail had received columns of newspaper coverage, Dolphin Beach being a relatively boring place, until recently. Most of the front pages of *The Dolphin Beach Free Press* had been devoted to the story; Amanda was featured in several editions, repeating her testimony with precise detail. I made copies of the more interesting articles, then left, turning the lights off behind me. I climbed the dark stairs, brushing dust from my dark skirt as I walked, and headed to the inn.

EIGHT

I WALKED INTO the bedroom, glanced longingly at the bed, and hurried into the bathroom. My body ached from a lack of sleep and the strain of fighting down emotions stirred up by the funeral. I stood under the shower, closed my eyes, waited for the hot water to revive me, and thought about the upcoming evening with pleasant anticipation. But as I shampooed my hair, a familiar feeling of dread began to creep over me.

Jeff had been killed thirty endless, pain-filled months ago. The bitterness and loss hadn't been dulled by the passing of nine hundred and twelve days. In spite of the encouragement of family and friends, I remained alone, preferring solitude to the dating game. "Great way to get psyched for a date." I turned the shower off and hurried to dry my hair and put on clothes and makeup. With luck, and green lights, I wouldn't be late.

Hugh's directions were easy to follow. I swung the car into the tree-lined driveway just as the sun was beginning to set, the tires crunching pleasantly on the gravel. I smiled and relaxed a little. Hugh eagerly bounded down the porch stairs and held the car door open. He took my arm and guided me to the house, happily chattering along the way. I was too exhausted to answer, but Hugh didn't notice.

Hugh's quick tour of the house expanded to a full-length excursion through passive energy-saving devices, convection ovens, and central air-conditioning. I made a furtive glance at my watch and unsuccessfully attempted to stifle a yawn.

Hugh noticed and blushed. "You've been here for ten minutes and I'm boring you already. The house was finished only a few months ago; I always forget that people aren't as excited about it as I am. Come on, let's go out back." He led me through the kitchen and slid open the glass doors. "I've been saving the best part for the end."

The view was postcard-perfect. The back porch was built high enough to provide an unobstructed view of the bay. Sailboats, making their way back to the marina before darkness, dotted the water. As if waiting for Hugh's cue, the sun sank below the horizon and threw flaming streaks of red and orange over the water. The dark waters of the bay reflected the vivid colors back into the sky. To complete the effect, a flock of seagulls flew across an orange plume and headed for home. I watched in awe and said, "Wow, did you plan this?"

"I saw the view and realized this was the perfect location for my dream house. Don't get me started again—I'll put you to sleep. How about a drink? Would you like beer, wine, or champagne?"

"Iced tea?"

He raised an eyebrow and excused himself. My offer to help was refused so I turned to watch the sailboats scurry across the bay. I let my guard down, and lethargy swept over me. I blinked tears back into my eyes and tried to forget everything—I'd worry tomorrow.

Hugh reappeared. He handed me a glass of tea and said, "You look beat; tough day?"

"Amanda's funeral was this morning." I placed the glass on the railing and closed my eyes, a vision of the burnished copper coffin instantly appeared inside my eyelids. "This was a mistake, I'm not going to be much fun tonight. It might be best for both of us if I just go back to the hotel."

There was a gentle pressure on my shoulders and the back of my neck. Hugh lightly massaged the knotted muscles and said, "Don't leave now. Being alone is the worst mistake you could make tonight." His fingers continued to knead my shoulders. "If you leave, you'll go sit in your dark hotel room, and get even more depressed. Please stay. You don't have to act like a happy guest. If you want to stand there and stare at the water until it's too dark to see anything, that's okay. If you want to talk, or cry, or rant and rave, that's okay too. At least stay and eat a little dinner. You'll feel better and I won't have to spend the evening worrying about you."

I didn't have the energy to answer or move. I shrugged.

"You know what your problem is? You're too tense; you've got to relax and just stop thinking for a little while. You could use a massage."

"What?" I opened my eyes and straightened up. "You must be kidding."

"I'm not kidding. When I was in med school, I worked as a masseur in a health club. I used to make extra money, or beer, by giving massages to the other students." He continued to rub my shoulders; I could feel the muscles relax slightly. "Doctor's orders..."

Hugh's magic line worked. Before I knew what was happening, I was lying on the bed, covered from the waist down with a sheet, and feeling exceptionally silly when he came into the bedroom. I looked at him over my shoulder and said, "Tell me, do other women fall for your massage line as easily as I did?"

"It's not a line. But I may start using it. This is going to feel a little cold at first." In spite of his warning, I jumped when the cold cream touched my naked back. A faint pine smell wafted through the room. I took a deep breath. Hugh said, "Ben Gay. I only use it for my special massages. Close your eyes and relax. Let me do the work."

It was good advice. I closed my eyes and concentrated on keeping all thoughts from my mind. Muscles and tendons loosened. Very gradually, I became acutely aware of his strong hands as they pressed against my shoulders, worked down my spine, and then retraced the path to my neck. His hands began another passage along my back, my skin rippling under his fingers. The tempo of his massage changed, his probing fingers became gentler, teasing. I shifted and lifted my back, and his hands slid under my arms and touched my breasts. He leaned closer and gently kissed the back of my neck. I shuddered, rolled over, and pulled him down to me.

A RUMBLING STOMACH and the smell of garlic woke me. Enough soft light fell in through the open doorway for me to find a maroon robe draped over a chair next to the bed. I put it on and pulled the belt tight; the sleeves were three or four inches too long. I rolled them up and walked out to the kitchen, following the garlic scent.

I walked into the kitchen, blinking in the harsh fluorescent light. Hugh was at the stove, also dressed in a robe. His was blue and he didn't need to roll the sleeves up. He looked at me and laughed. "You look like a sleepy owl."

I yawned, pushed a few strands of errant hair back into place, and said, "I can't believe I fell asleep. What time is it?"

"Almost nine-thirty." He laughed again. "You didn't even stay awake long enough to smoke the proverbial cigarette. I didn't have the heart to wake you up; you looked so peaceful. But I finally got hungry. I was hoping the garlic would bring you around. And if that didn't work, I was going to take desperate measures and wave a plate of spaghetti under your nose. And if that didn't work, I was planning on uttering a loud sigh—and eating by myself. I'm glad I didn't have to do all that."

We didn't talk much during dinner. My thoughts drifted off. I realized Hugh was waiting for an answer to a question he had asked. I blushed and looked confused. He laughed and said, "You really haven't been listening to me. I was suggesting that we have our coffee in the living room: too many bugs outside."

Hugh refused my offer to help him clean the dishes, led me into the living room, and settled me on the couch. He apologized and promised to return as soon as the dishes were scraped and in the dishwasher.

Under normal circumstances, I would have insisted on helping or taken the opportunity to snoop around, looking at the bookcases and record shelves; you can tell a lot about a person from their taste in music and books. But not tonight. I made a feeble attempt to get up and failed. My last thought was that Miss Manners would not be pleased with dinner guests who fell asleep on the sofa while the host was washing the dishes. The fear of Miss Manners' disapproval wasn't strong enough to rouse me; I fell asleep.

I PANICKED. Flinging aside the afghan that was covering me, I struggled against the soft cushions to an upright position. Disoriented by the unfamiliar surroundings, I cradled my head in my hands, moaned softly, and tried to bring myself out of the nightmare. After a few minutes I was able to control the panting and shivering. I knew further sleep would be impossible; the intensity of the nightmare would stay with me for hours.

The walls of the living room contracted, restricting the supply of fresh air; I had to get outside. Mimicking Linus and his security blanket, I pulled the bathrobe around me and padded off to the porch, dragging the afghan behind me. I moved a chair to the railing, wrapping myself in the blanket to fight off the autumnal chill signaling the approaching end of summer. Once securely bundled up, I sat down, stretched my legs out on the railing, and lit a cigarette....

THE SCREEN DOOR slid open. Of course it was Hugh. Somehow, I'd been expecting him.

"I thought I heard a noise out here. Are you okay?" The concern in his voice was unmistakable but I wasn't ready to talk. I nodded, wishing he would go away and leave me to my solitary misery. He didn't leave. He ignored my hostile body language, sat down on the railing, and asked, "Cold?"

I took a deep drag on the cigarette, held it, and then let the words and smoke slowly trickle out. "No, it feels good to be outside and not get soaked."

"I didn't know you smoke."

I took another drag, held the butt between my thumb and index finger, and stared at the glowing red tip. The smoke hung in the still air. "I don't usually smoke a lot. It's not good for my running, but I'm not ready to give it up. I'm working on getting rid of one bad habit at a time."

"Judging from that pile of butts in the ashtray, you've been out here working on this bad habit for quite a while. It's almost 4:00 A.M. How long have you been sitting out here?''

"A couple hours. I went in once to get more cigarettes and"—I wiggled my toes—"to steal a pair of your socks from the laundry room. Hope you don't mind; my feet were cold.''

He wanted to ask, "What's the matter with you?" But instead, he very politely said, "Couldn't sleep?''

"No, I couldn't sleep." I violently stabbed the cigarette into the ashtray, almost knocking it from my lap. "I'm sorry. My sense of humor seems to have disappeared." I ran my fingers through my hair, picking out words that wouldn't sound harsh. "I had another nightmare and couldn't get back to sleep. I came out for some fresh air.''

With clinical detachment, Hugh said, "Another nightmare. Do you have them often?''

"It, not them. I always have the same dream.... I wake up in the middle of the night, calling Jeff's name. Jeff is—was—my husband. He was killed almost three years ago." I lit another cigarette and let out a shaky breath. "He worked for the government and was killed during a drug raid." My matter-of-fact voice quavered. I struggled to regain a monotone and went on. "I wake up and reach across the bed for him. He's not there—he never is. The bed is empty. I panic. Then I remember, ... I turn over, bury my face in the pillows, and tell myself to go back to sleep. It takes a long time, but I manage to fall asleep." The cigarette was burning steadily. I watched the cheerful red glow and said, "That's when the nightmare begins.''

All the bottled up words spilled out. "It's night. I'm standing in a foggy clearing, the type you see in a low-budget horror movie, where the mist swirls around the star, obscuring her vision. It's hot and unbearably humid. My clothes are sticking to me. I'm hot, sweaty, and very nervous. There's a pond behind me; the crickets and bullfrogs are so loud, I can't hear anything else. I know someone is watching me, but I can't see anyone. I'm lost and on the edge of panic. A clearing is before me; the road is beyond it. I must get to that road; it leads to safety but I'm afraid to walk into that open space and be exposed—to what I don't know—but I have to get to the road."

The terror of the dream returned. I pulled the afghan around my shoulders and tried to steady myself. Hugh rested his hand on my leg and said, "Take your time. You're okay now."

"I step into the field. My sneakers are wet from the dew. Nothing happens. I keep walking. Twenty or thirty feet from the road, a figure jumps out from behind a tree. It's a man. He shoots and misses. My pistol is in my hand; I shoot. He falls to the ground. Another shadowy figure pops up, firing as he jumps to his feet. The same things happens. He misses; I don't. It happens again and again. My ammunition is going to run out and I start to worry. My gun jams. Another man jumps up and aims a huge gun at me. He's too close: he won't miss. Desperate, I yank on the trigger until it fires, the man falls to the ground. My knees buckle. I collapse and crawl to the body, curious to see his face. The fog disappears. A bright light floods the field, shining directly on the body—it's Jeff. His sightless eyes are turned toward me. I scream and scream and scream until my voice disappears. A baby's cry cuts through my shock. I roll aside my husband's corpse and uncover a small infant. The crying grows fainter and fainter; the infant dies while I watch helplessly.''

The image was too vivid. I stopped to blow my nose and pull another cigarette from the crumpled pack. I lit the cigarette and quietly said, ''I was almost three months pregnant when Jeff died. A few weeks after the funeral I lost the baby.'' Hugh groaned and tightened his grip on my leg.

''My screams usually wake me. I'm shaking, crying, and drenched in sweat. Tonight was different. I managed to wake myself before I started screaming. I don't even try to go back to sleep.''

''So you sit up the rest of the night and smoke cigarettes?''

I looked at the cigarette in my hand. ''Yes. I smoke cigarettes and tell myself I'll survive this—I just need more time. Smoking is an improvement. A few months ago, I would smoke and drink until I passed out. For almost two years I drank. Deep inside, even during my worst binges, I knew drinking was only a temporary salve for the pain. Not a good solution, but the only one I could find. Finally, I couldn't fool myself any longer; it was time to stop hiding in a bottle, time to face reality again.''

I took one last drag on the latest cigarette and quickly exhaled. ''It's been a struggle. Every night I'm tempted to crawl back into that alcoholic haze. I constantly remind myself: 'You chose reality.' Some nights I lie awake in bed repeating that phrase into the empty darkness. Other nights, like tonight, I'm not sure reality was the right choice. I never had nightmares when I was drunk...."

Hugh knelt in front of the chair and put his arms around me. He held me until I stopped shivering, said, "Let's go to bed," and pulled me to my feet. I followed him to the bedroom and drifted off to sleep, my head safely nestled against his chest.

NINE

THE UNUSUAL SENSATION of warm sunlight on my face woke me. I lay under the sheet, enjoying the warmth and the sight of Hugh asleep by my side. I stroked the blond hair curling on his chest, anxious to continue last night's encounter. But I pulled my hand back, too guilty to interrupt his deep sleep. I had fallen asleep on him—not once, but twice—and then kept him awake until dawn with my nightmare stories. I decided to let him sleep.

The sunshine was too beautiful to ignore. I slipped out of the bed, fished a bathrobe from the tangled heap on the floor, put it on, and went out to the car for the extra set of running clothes I stash in the back.

I started off with the good intentions of a long, slow workout, determined to enjoy the early morning quiet. My good intentions vanished after a few miles as my mind traveled through the past four days. My casual pace increased. Those four days had caught me in a crazy whirlwind, forcing me into the unaccustomed and uncomfortable role of a spectator, reacting to the events exploding around me.

I had too many unconnected suspicions, too many questions and not enough time. My legs and chest protested against too many cigarettes and not enough sleep. I slowed to an easy jog, caught my breath, and turned back to the house.

Hugh was sitting on the back deck, drinking from a large mug; a thermos and matching mug sat on the table next to him. He waited until I climbed the stairs, smiled, and said, "So you decided to come back. When I woke up and found your side of the bed empty, I thought I had scared you away. But when I got up and discovered your car sitting in the driveway, I knew you'd be back. Want some coffee? Did you have a good run? How far did you go?"

"About eight miles. And yes to the coffee." I sat on the stairs, kicked off my running shoes, and peeled the damp socks from my feet. "I opened my eyes, saw the sun, and was too excited to stay in bed." I accepted the mug of coffee, and the kiss, he offered.

"You taste sweaty," was his comment after ending the long, promising kiss.

"Thanks." I wiped sweat from my forehead. "Do I smell bad too?" I took a sip of the coffee and remembered my resolution to be a better person. "Hugh, about last night, I'm sorry—"

Hugh held up a hand. "Don't apologize." He grinned. "The beginning of the evening was rough; but I sure enjoyed the way it ended. Don't get too excited about the sunshine; the weather reports say another storm is going to hit soon." He stood up and offered me a hand. "How about breakfast?"

I got to my feet. "Cooking isn't one of my favorite pastimes, but I do make great omelets. If you can wait until after I take a shower, I'll make you a breakfast worth waiting for."

He gravely considered my offer and then said, "Okay, you can cook. But only if you let me wash your back...."

It was almost noon before we got around to breakfast.

HOLLIS WILSON, C.P.A., looked at me with annoyance. Instead of snapping, "You still here?" he apologized and promised to keep me waiting for only another ten or fifteen minutes. The fifteen minutes stretched to twenty, then twenty-five.

The old journals and magazines scattered around the waiting room didn't hold my attention for long. I prowled around the waiting room and stopped to examine the pictures on the wall behind the vacant receptionist's desk. The papers on the desk caught my attention; I leafed through them.

Bills, all of them unpaid, were in the stack. Some were politely stamped, "Second Notice" or carried the notation, "In case you overlooked..."; a few had cute cartoons depicting unhappy characters waiting for payment. All of the notes requested immediate attention; a few threatened legal action.

I pulled out my notebook, wrote down the social security numbers, dropped the dunning notices back on the desk, and turned to look at the pictures. Wilson walked out and motioned for me to follow, talking as we walked into his office. "Boyd Johnson tells me you're working for his insurance company. Says you people think he killed Amanda. Now I told Boyd you're simply trying to do your job. No need for him to get riled up at you or that insurance company.

Wilson eased me into a battered chair and said, "Now, you just give me a minute or two and I'll go take a peek at that file. Didn't have a chance to look for it this morning. My secretary is sick; things are a little disorganized." He left the room.

As soon as he left, I stood up and walked around the office, disappointed because the top of his desk was clear. The appointment book was empty; business was not good. The bookshelves were crammed with dusty, little-used tax journals. Hollis was a dedicated family man. The wall behind his desk was covered with family pictures; kids, dogs, horses, and assorted relatives were framed in haphazard, slightly out-of-focus poses.

Wilson reentered the room, file in hand. "Here it is. Uhh, uhh, uhh..." He examined the file and snapped it shut. "Nothing unusual. Tell your insurance company to stop worrying. I recommended the increase in the coverage, in light of the rapid growth of their company. Key man insurance..."

The accountant sat back in his chair, prepared to deliver a long lecture on the benefits of key man—his word, not mine—insurance. I stopped him and recited, "Insurance on employees vital to the operation is taken out by the company, with the company as beneficiary, to protect itself from the financial loss that would be suffered if that key employee should die. I'm very well acquainted with the concept."

He was disappointed to have an opportunity to display his knowledge canceled. "Well, okay, although I guess you womanlibbers call it key person insurance." I let his remark pass; I'd leave the consciousness-raising to someone else. "CIG reviewed, and approved, the application. Nothing extraordinary." He peered over his bifocals and said, "Now young lady"—I winced at the term—"I don't understand the problem. In my opinion, your insurance company does not have reasonable grounds for delaying payment of the death benefit."

"I'm sure you realize an investigation is standard procedure." I was getting tired of repeating that phrase. "Surely you don't expect the insurance company to send off a check without taking some time to get the facts; that wouldn't be prudent." I was having trouble understanding why people expected "my" insurance company to cheerfully send off five and a half million dollars without question.

"I'd like to ask you a few questions." He nodded but his answers were evasive. I lost patience, stood up, and ended the interview by saying, "Thank you for your time. I appreciate your help and can assure you that I'm doing everything possible to expedite"— accountants like to hear that kind of talk—"the investigation."

The entire visit had been a waste of time. Instinctively, I knew the rest of the day wouldn't be any different. I'd waste my time asking people the questions they expected to hear and listen to the answers I expected to hear. I wouldn't learn anything new or helpful, unless I could startle someone into blurting out an honest answer.

Wilson escorted me to the door, relief that I was leaving shining on his face. I stopped and asked, "Were the Johnsons having marital problems?"

The question caught him off guard; his relief deflated. It appeared as if this was going to be one of those lucky occasions when the truth slips out. Hollis precariously teetered on the verge of an honest answer. He quickly regained his balance; the lizardlike eyes blinked. "I can assure you we never had any discussions relating to divorce."

"Did I mention divorce? Were they considering a divorce?"

He jabbed his index finger in the air, stiffly pointing it at my chest, and with righteous indignation said, "If you continue to proceed in this tawdry vein, you and the Canfield Insurance Group will have to answer for it. I will not allow you to roam around this town, uttering ugly insinuations and false accusations about Boyd and Amanda Johnson."

"Wait a second!" I raised my voice to match his. "My questions are not out of line. If I offended you, I am sorry. I am also sorry that Amanda Johnson is dead. Thank you for your help!" The door slammed behind me; I'd made another friend in Dolphin Beach.

It may be unethical—I never stopped to consider the legality—nor did I care to solicit Eileen's opinion. During the past few years, I had carefully, and expensively, cultivated friendships at several major credit bureaus. It was time to take advantage of those friendships. I wanted to know more about the stack of unpaid bills in Wilson's office. One quick telephone call from a booth near Wilson's office was enough; I'd have a credit report before tomorrow morning's talk shows ended.

CRUMBLING PIERS, abandoned warehouses, and run-down tenements lined the waterfront section of Dolphin Beach that was unimaginatively known as the Docks. It was the part of town tourists never ventured into; the part of town omitted from the Chamber of Commerce walking-tour map. Far removed from the santized, antiseptic Victorians; tourist dollars would never travel there.

Perry King lived in the center of the Docks. I left the Porsche sedately parked in a public lot blocks away, foolishly hoping to be less conspicuous without the car. Who was I kidding? Lady Godiva riding bareback down Fifth Avenue at noon on a hot summer day would attract less attention.

People, young and old, male and female, hung out on what those of us who grew up in New York City called the stoop. Boom boxes blasted rap music into the humid air, teenaged mothers rocked their babies to the beat, old men and older women shared gossip and beer from cans hidden in brown paper bags. Everyone fell silent as I approached. Every eye followed my progress; conversations resumed only after I was safely past. I hurried along the litter-strewn avenue, praying for invisibility, or safe passage, not sure which was more unlikely.

My hope of being less noticeable on foot grew more insane with each step. This was one of the worst ideas I had managed to dream up in quite some time. It was easily the leading candidate for "Worst Idea of the Year." And I'd had quite a few bad ideas this year. I longed for the obscurity of the Porsche. In it, I'd blend into the neighborhood, look like one of the customers pulling up to the curb to ~~reach~~ ~~my~~ supply of whatever illegal substance I wanted to inject or smoke—everything was available.

Pimps, prostitutes, and pushers stared. Every drunk called out obscene suggestions; every beggar stuck out a grimy hand and cursed as I walked past, leaving him with empty hands. I ignored everyone and everything—especially the sweat rolling down my back— and cautioned myself against showing fear. I forced myself to walk slower, gaining small comfort from the pistol under my arm.

I reached the relative safety of the house where King lived and allowed myself to relax, a little—the house did not exactly inspire confidence. Salt air and blowing sand had ground the paint off, exposing dusty sepia boards. I walked up the stairs, barely managed to avoid a gaping hole in the rotted porch. The landlady's surly, "He ain't here," was my reward for navigating the decaying staircase without mishap.

Coaxing, cajoling, and twenty dollars convinced her I wasn't a cop out to harm her friend Perry. An arthritic hand pushed open the screen door; grimy fingers snatched the bill from my hand. She pulled the door closed and examined the twenty before saying, "Perry's a good man. He made a bad mistake. He done his time. You got no business pestering him, stirring up old trouble."

"Yes, ma'am." I spoke into the torn screen; the dim outline of a short, thin woman was all that could be seen behind the dirty mesh.

A long-forgotten childhood memory of kneeling in a darkened confessional, reciting a carefully re-hearsed list of sins to the disembodied voice of a priest floating out from behind a black silk veil, flashed in my mind. One Saturday afternoon temptation and curiosity overpowered me; I lifted that little piece of silk and excitedly peered beneath it, expecting to be struck dead, just reward for my blasphemous action. God didn't seem to notice; an ordinary screen was all I found under that mysterious cloth.

I assumed the sincere tone that used to work in the confessional and said, "I'm not going to make trou-ble for Perry. I need to ask him a few questions and maybe keep him out of trouble. Where can I find him?"

"Perry's at the Mission. Nobody except them would take a chance on an ex-con..." She rambled on; I lis-tened patiently and patiently extracted directions be-fore picking my way down the ramshackle stairs, back out into the bright sunlight, 98 degrees, 98 percent humidity.

A TINY SIGN, hanging in the dirt-streaked window of an ex-supermarket, identified the building as The Mission. Wondering what, or who, the Mission was,

I struggled with the heavy door, hoped to be greeted with an icy blast from an air conditioner, and was disappointed to find ceiling fans struggling to circulate the heavy, damp air.

In response to my question, an elderly janitor pointed to a set of doors in the rear of the large, empty room. "Perry's in the kitchen." My heels clicked on the tile floors, echoing in the vacant hall; long lines of tables and chairs were the only occupants. Religious posters, first aid information, and discarded travel agency posters of picturesque beaches and snow-capped mountains hung on the bare cinder-block walls, vain attempts to brighten the dingy gray.

I pushed through the swinging door, my footsteps drowned out by the clatter of metal as a tray of silverware was dumped into a sink. A man, tall enough to play center on any professional basketball team, looked up from behind the double sink. I'd seen enough pictures of Perry King during yesterday's marathon library session to recognize him without an introduction.

He lifted a handful of forks from the soapy water and rinsed them. He nodded to acknowledge my presence and said, "You don't look like a health inspector. Can I help you?"

I was taken aback by his courteous tone and immediately ashamed for expecting less. I recovered and said, "I'm sorry to barge in without warning, but it's important. I have to ask you a few questions about Amanda Johnson."

If King noticed my momentry confusion, he chose to ignore it and asked, "You a reporter? 'Cause I don't have anything to say to reporters. Just write 'no comment' next to my name and leave me alone to do my work. Sorry, lady, you're going to have to find some other way to sell your newspapers; I'm not going to help you write a little exclusive interview."

"I'm not a reporter." I held out a card and introduced myself. "I'm an investigator."

It was his turn to hide a startled expression. He ignored the card and said, "You don't look like a cop. Did Price send you down here?"

"Wrong again." I grinned. "I'm not a cop and I'm certainly not working for Price. We've met; he's a jerk." As an afterthought, I added, "He doesn't like me either. I'm a private investigator."

"If Price doesn't like you, you must be okay." King dried his hands on the towel that was casually draped over a shoulder. He accepted the business card I was still holding out and slipped it into the breast pocket of his sweaty shirt. "It's about time for a break. Come on, let's go out back and have a smoke; you can ask your questions there."

King led me through a storeroom filled with shelves of institutional sized cans of government surplus vegetables, beef stew, fruit cocktail, and peanut butter. We walked out onto a loading dock. King pulled two metal chairs from the kitchen and opened them up under the shady overhang of the roof.

We both lit cigarettes. I broke the silence and asked, "Who runs the Mission? Your sign doesn't offer much information."

"We aren't affiliated wtih any particular religion. Our programs are a cooperative effort, funded by several of the town's churches, synagogues, and a few businesses. The name is deliberately vague to avoid identification with any religion. We also receive some funding from the United Way, but their resources are stretched pretty thin."

He shrugged with resignation. "Our resources are pretty limited too. I'm the chief cook and bottle-washer. Usually that's a joke, but not today. The director gets to lend a hand." He examined his chapped hands. "No one at the Mission is impressed with titles—too much to do. Our clientele is pretty varied. We do the best we can for anyone who walks in through our doors. Give 'em a good meal, arrange for some counseling, medical care, maybe help find a job—but those are pretty scarce around here. Some days all we can do is provide a little acceptance and a friendly ear. A hell of a lot of people have dropped into that black hole where those who don't have enough money to pay for the help they need but are too rich to 'qualify' for government aid fall. We try to help pull some of those people out of those holes."

He flicked his cigarette butt into the weeds of the overgrown parking lot. I followed his lead, fished my pack out of my jacket pocket, and offered it to him. "Sure, I've got time for one more—especially if it's yours." I lit a match as he continued to talk. "I guess you know Amanda Johnson got me this job."

The match burned my fingertips. I dropped it and exclaimed, "What?"

"Sorry." He grinned. "I guess you didn't know." His apology was less than sincere. "Amanda was a member of the board of directors. She knew I was getting out of prison and asked me if I'd like to accomplish something worthwhile with my M.B.A. I did. Amanda persuaded the other board members to take a chance and hire me. Amanda was a very persuasive lady; she convinced them I'd be a good role model for our clients. We're going to miss her."

We both stared at the weeds breaking through the asphalt. King took a final drag on the cigarette and spun it out into the air. "Two cigarettes is a long break; I have to get back inside. What did you want to ask? Must be important to get you to come alone to this part of town."

"Ahh . . ." I blushed, too embarrassed to admit the true purpose behind my visit. "Never mind; you already answered it."

"Oh." He grinned again. "The police have already asked me that question; they weren't nearly as considerate as you. On the night Amanda was killed, I was out of town at a conference. Yes, plenty of witnesses will swear to seeing me at that meeting. No, the big black ex-convict did not kill the petite white woman who sent him to jail." Resignation, not anger, permeated his voice; he stood up, decisively ending our discussion. "But thank you for not asking."

"Where was this conference?"

"Wilmington." We stared at each other for a few seconds, King finally breaking the deadlock. "I have to get back inside. Call if you have more questions."

He walked me to the front door. The kitchen was now bustling with activity; a cooking crew had appeared, clanging pots and pans and trading raucous insults as they prepared the meal. After learning that I'd arrived on foot, King insisted on calling a taxi. "It's going to be dark soon; this is not the neighborhood for a pretty lady to walk through alone."

A taxi pulled up to the curb, King held open the door, and said, "Stop by any time. You'll have to come back for the dedication ceremony." Seeing the blank look on my face, he explained, "Amanda not only gave us a lot of her valuable time, she also left us a sizable bequest. Amanda wanted to fund a shelter for battered wives; it was a special interest of hers. The board wants to dedicate the shelter to her memory." He patted his breast pocket. "We'll send you an invitation; I have your address."

TEN

THE BEACH MOBILE Home Park lived up to its advertising; it was close to the beach. If you listened carefully and ignored the televisions and radios blaring out from the open doors—not many residents had air-conditioning—the sound of the ocean was almost audible. Noise and light spilled out from the doorways. I caught glimpses of men in their shorts, and women in wrinkled cotton housedresses, sitting motionless in front of glowing television screens. Laugh tracks provided background noise for life in the park.

The park was a planner's nightmare. A straight blacktop road cut through the center of the plot. Short cul-de-sacs, each identified by flowery names, intersected the road; identical trailers sat at forty-five degree angles to the street.

The posted speed limit was fifteen miles per hour. I drove much slower, squinting at each street sign, trying to spot Tulip Court. Stopping at the office, another silver trailer, for directions would have made sense, but I passed it by; I didn't want to attract attention. I had even taken the extreme measure of leaving the Porsche safely parked (I hoped) in the airport parking lot; it didn't seem to be a suitable vehicle to cruise a trailer park without attracting notice. So I traded it in for a nondescript sedan from a rental agency; the radio wasn't very good but I wouldn't complain—the air conditioner worked.

Azalea Court, Begonia Place, Carnation Court, Dogwood Terrace, the flowers fell in alphabetical order until I reached Tulip Court. Slip D was carefully outlined with tulips, bordered by a neat row of seashells. Tulip season was over; I bent and touched the petals—they were plastic.

This mobile home was air-conditioned; the steady hum of a motor, struggling to fight the humidity, muffled my tentative knock on the aluminum door. I banged a little harder. The door cracked open. "It's Blaine Stewart. I need to talk with you." The woman peering out tried to slam the door but couldn't; my foot was securely wedged into the narrow opening.

"Go away before somebody sees you. If they find out I talked to you, I'll get fired." Her plea failed; I didn't move. "Go away, please..."

"Not until we talk."

"You don't understand; it's not easy to find work in this town. I don't have anyone to take care of me. My job at BAJ pays a good salary; if they let me go I'll wind up as a cashier in a gift shop down by the harbor. Maybe, if I'm lucky, I'll be able to find work as a waitress. They make good tips during the summer." Her voice trembled. "I'm too old to start over in a minimum wage job."

She pushed against the door; the pressure on my sneaker added urgency to my voice. "Louise, how many years did you know Amanda? Six? Seven? Amanda told me you always called her your daughter. Are you going to cower behind that door and let your daughter's murder go unpunished because you're afraid of getting fired?'' The pressure on my foot eased slightly. "I won't go away; you'll have to call the police to get rid of me."

The door opened. I hurried into the metal house before she could change her mind. The hallway was narrow and cramped with bookshelves; Louise turned and silently led me into the living room/dining room/ bedroom. It was a studio trailer, about the same size as the average New York City apartment. I felt at home.

Louise found the remote control and abruptly snapped the television off. "Sit down," was her inhospitable invitation.

The choices were limited: sofa bed or rocking chair. I settled into the rocking chair and looked around. Louise didn't have much furniture, but she managed to amass an impressive collection of ceramic animals. Poodles, rabbits, bears, penguins, and giraffes stared at me from the shelves. Not a speck of dust was visible; a lot of free time must be devoted to polishing the silent menagerie.

She plucked a collie from a bookcase, stood in the center of the room, and stroked the porcelain dog's head. "You don't know how many times I started to call your office to leave a message for you to get in touch with me. But I always hung up. And now you turn up on my front lawn...."

"Who threatened to fire you? Was it Mr. Johnson?"

"No." She tightened her hold on the dog. "Jennifer—you remember her—she's Mr. Johnson's secretary. She said Mr. Johnson told her no one should cooperate with your investigation because you were just trying to cause trouble. And he would cause trouble for anyone who connived with you."

The woman was frightened. We watched each other. Did I have any moral obligation not to drag her in deeper? I considered the question for a few seconds. And decided.

"Louise, I don't want to cause trouble for anybody but the person who killed Amanda." She fumbled in the pocket of her housedress for a tissue. "We never finished the conversation we started in the cafeteria. Did you ever overhear any conversations between the Johnsons about business?" Her eyes shifted from mine to the floor. I rocked forward: Maybe business wasn't as good as Boyd proclaimed. "How is the new hardware division doing?"

Louise looked up and asked, "You've seen the BAJpc1000?" I had seen pictures of the new computer. I nodded. "The sales have been good, better than expected. We've been having trouble keeping up with the demand. No one has said anything officially but a lot of rumors are going around. The factory can't keep up with orders. Dealers are calling, screaming for their back orders. The factory in Taiwan has been having labor problems: strikes and slowdowns...."

She unconsciously shifted to the company line. "We've been working real hard on the backlog. We should be caught up soon. I heard Mr. Johnson tell that to Mrs. Johnson. He said to her, 'Don't worry. I'm on top of the situation.' That's what he said to her on Monday.''

Monday, Amanda's last day in the office. ''What else did you hear?''

''Nothing much. Mrs. Johnson said something about the reports, and Mr. Johnson closed the door. Mrs. Johnson left soon after that. It was the last time I saw her.''

10:32. THE CAR WAS mine until noon tomorrow, more than enough time to explore the nightlife at the Docks and maybe learn more about Amanda's cocaine connection. But first I pulled into a Hardee's restaurant parking lot and unsnapped my shoulder holster. The Docks had been a frightening experience in the bright daylight; I wasn't going to make a nighttime visit without being fully prepared. I checked to be sure the pistol's ammunition clip was full and slipped it under the seat where it would be instantly accessible before I drove any deeper into the combat zone. The Docks were a popular destination this Tuesday night; the bland car easily blended into a long line of expensive foreign cars, family sedans, and kids in their parents' borrowed station wagons.

Ten short blocks formed the battleground. The cruising pattern was simple: drive north on Harbour Drive, pass the XXX-rated movie theaters, porn shops advertising activities unimaginable to most people, and twenty-four-hour grocery stores, to Sand Hill

Lane. Turn left. Make an immediate left turn onto First Avenue. First is boring, no action. Gun the engine, and race ten blocks to Inlet Road. Make a quick left and then another left to Harbour Drive. The loop was complete—you're back on Harbour Drive where anything, legal or illegal, is for sale.

The one-way street made it easy for prospective buyers to inspect and complete their purchases. People intrested in buying hard goods—drugs, guns, and other assorted illegal objects—parked on the left side of the broad avenue. Those interested in soft goods— hookers or drugs—looked to the right. Prostitutes, male, female, and some whose sex was not readily apparent in the uneven light, posed on the boardwalk, waiting for a cruising car to park and its driver beckon.

It was a drive-through business. Buyers cruised the circuit, examining the merchandise. When a decision was made, the driver swerved out of the parade and glided to the curb. Drug sales were completed within minutes. Money and narcotics were exchanged, the transaction was completed, and the car drove away. The prostitutes took longer; one would approach the waiting auto, enter into negotiations, and finally slip into the passenger seat. The car would ease back into traffic, heading to an isolated parking lot with an ocean view.

After three circuits, I knew the layout and the process. I also knew the next logical step was to stop and play the role of prospective customer. But I couldn't bring myself to do it; the thought of parking and talking with the dealing scum was repulsive. Memories of bungled deals were too painful for me to contemplate getting involved in that business again.

I lit a cigarette and decided to make one more trip around; maybe a brilliant idea would strike as I drove. Not one appeared. I turned back onto Harbour Drive. Three-quarters of the way down the strip, I took a deep breath and dropped out of the procession.

An eager young tradesman sauntered across the sidewalk. I rolled the window down, humidity slapping my face. "Hey lady, what you looking for? I got everything. Good prices too. You new here: I'll give you my first-time buyer special. Whatever you want, I got the best."

A deep baritone yelled, "What the hell are you doing?" A man stepped out from the shadows and ran to the car.

Shit, a cop! I prayed the gun was hidden from sight and waited.

"Jamie." The man grabbed the kid and yanked him away from the car. "Man, don't you have any brains? Dammit, you're on probation. This could get you tossed back in jail, and no fancy lawyer will be able to get you out this time."

"And you—" The man peered in the window to turn his wrath on me. It was Perry King; he recognized me and was not happy. "What the fuck are you doing out here? Didn't you do enough sightseeing this afternoon? What's the matter, lady, your stash gone? Well, you're not buying any shit from Jamie; he's out of business."

Perry's glare swung from Jamie to me and back to the frightened teenager. I interrupted the tirade. "I'm not buying. I wanted to ask him a few questions."

King wasn't satisfied; he stuck his head in the car window and barked out an order. "You wait here. I'll be right back—give you all the answers you want."

He dragged Jamie away from the curb to the vacant lot and forced the boy to empty his pockets. A wad of cash came out first. Perry looked at the roll and stuck it into his pocket. A small paper bag came out next. King peered into the brown sack, walked over to the sewer, and threw the contents into the storm drain, ignoring Jamie's protests. Perry dismissed the boy with a few sharp words.

Jamie scurried into the night. King took three angry strides to the passenger's side of the car, jerked the door open, and jumped in. He was barely able to control his temper. "Shit, lady, are you crazy? You could get hurt down here—or worse. You got questions? You ask me; don't try to get one of my people involved. Let's get out of here. There's a little beach a couple miles down the road. No one will bother us there."

I started the car and drove down the street. "I don't need your lectures. I can take care of myself." He didn't answer, so I asked a question. "What are you doing? Running a one-man crusade to clean up the neighborhood?"

"No crusade. These people are my clients. Jamie is a miserable kid who still has the potential to make something good of himself. I'm trying to keep him out of trouble. He's lucky you're not a cop."

We didn't attempt small talk. After a mile or two Perry pointed to a parking lot entrance and said, "Pull in there." I followed his instructions and put the car in park—it was too humid to turn off the air conditioner—and I turned to face King. I grabbed a pack of cigarettes from the dashboard and offered one to him. Once the cigarettes were lit King said, "What do you want to know?"

What did I want to know? Two cigarette tips glowed in the dark car. I watched them, carefully phrasing my response. "I want to know about the drugs in this town. Who's supplying, where it's coming from, and who's protecting the dealers?"

Perry replied with one low word. "Why?"

"My client is interested."

"Who's your client?" When I didn't answer, King said, "Do you think Amanda Johnson's death is related to drugs?"

"Maybe, maybe not. I won't know until I get a better handle on what's happening in this town."

"Would you tell me if you did think drugs were involved?"

"No. I wouldn't be in business very long if I told people my reasons for asking questions. You wouldn't talk to me if you thought I would repeat whatever you told me to the first person who asked. I may not be very smart, but I don't repeat stories." Without pausing, I said, "What was Jamie selling tonight?"

"Lightning. It's the local brand of cocaine."

Brand names for crack and cocaine were common-place in New York and other large cities. I was surprised to find that level of sophistication had penetrated the rural South. "What other brands are available?"

"None. Something called Thunderbolt was around for a while but it disappeared about a year ago. Lightning has total control of the market. Let me give you some advice. You could get into serious trouble by asking too many questions 'bout things like cocaine."

"Skip the lecture. What's your connection?"

"My only connection is geographic. I'm trying to keep my clients out of trouble. As for the drugs, it's a very well organized business. No competition, no fighting over turf, and no violence. The supply is constant and endless; the police don't care. They don't bother to come here until the concerned citizens complain. Then the cops come around, bust a few pushers and yank a few prostitutes off the boardwalk for the evening. After a few days, and a lot of newspaper and television coverage, the cops and the outraged citizens lose interest. The patrols ease off, and it's back to business as usual. Peaceful coexistence as long as the trash remains in its proper district."

"Where does the supply come from?"

Perry shrugged. "Who knows? This is a sea town; it's easy to run your boat down to Colombia, load your cargo, sail back up, unload, package it, and truck it out to the rest of the country. It's a short drive to the Interstate. Once you get on I-95, you're on your way to all the big cities, New York, D.C., Boston. Dolphin Beach is a great location; there are hundreds of inlets where a shipment can be unloaded. Fishing has been bad lately; lots of local boys would be tempted by the easy money.''

''You're pretty knowledgeable—''

''Lady,'' he interrupted. ''I'm an ex-convict. I spend eighteen to twenty hours a day trying to salvage the wreckage that floats up to the Mission. Of course I know what's going on down here. Anybody could easily figure it out.''

''Hey, don't misunderstand me. I'm not accusing you of being involved. I was going to ask if you ever heard a woman named Jessica mentioned in connection with the drug business.''

I wished the light from the streetlights was brighter so I could read the expression on Perry's face. ''Not too many ladies running cocaine down here.'' Suspicion entered his voice. ''Why are you so interested in cocaine? I thought you were a P.I. investigating a murder; maybe I was wrong. Maybe you're trying to cut your own deal. Maybe you're a narc.''

The accusation made me uneasy. I answered and was surprised by my vehemence. ''I really don't care to get involved in Dolphin Beach's drug problems. Drugs ruined my life, but I'm not planning to start a one-woman rampage to eradicate them from the face of the earth. My motives are less pure; I want to find Amanda's killer, then get out of here and forget this damn town.''

Perry didn't respond. He opened the car door and said, ''Let me give you a little friendly advice. You don't know the people around here; this is a tight community. These folks don't take too kindly to strangers. You start prowling around, asking the wrong people the wrong questions, and you'll find yourself in deep shit. Keep away from the Docks before you get hurt. You could wind up dead—other people have." He slid out into the night.

MY PLANS TO WRITE case notes were forgotten when I walked into the bedroom and saw the bed. My aching body demanded sleep. I peeled off my clothes and tossed them on the floor; the makeup could wait until morning. I collapsed on the bed and was asleep before the sheet settled around my shoulders.

The nightmarish sound of a ringing telephone jolted me awake. The room was dark, my heart was pounding—phone calls in the middle of the night always bring bad news. The people with good news wait for daylight.

I fumbled in the darkness for the telephone and hoped I would be able to get rid of the caller quickly, before I woke up completely. I found the receiver, dropped it, and finally managed to find my ear.

"Blaine?"

Still groggy from the shattered deep sleep, I didn't recognize the voice. I said, "Who is this? . . ." and realized it was my sister. "Oh, Eileen, what's up?"

"Yes, it's Eileen. Don't you bother to return calls anymore?"

She was mad and I didn't know why. So I asked, "What time is it?" to gain time to wake up and start thinking.

"One twenty-three to be precise. What happened? I left a message."

"Wait a second. Eileen, let's not start this conversation with the same argument we had last time we talked. I haven't been sleeping much lately. I came in and collapsed on the bed without checking for messages." I was pleased with my diplomatic approach to her anger. "I'm sorry I missed your call. Was it important?"

"Yes!" hissed through the receiver. "I spent the entire afternoon and part of this evening with Stan Adams—defending you."

My stomach sank through the mattress to the floor. I didn't answer, whatever I said would be wrong. Eileen didn't need prompting from me to continue; she could barely restrain her temper. "We have been fired."

I sat up in the bed, totally and completely awake. My answer wasn't very articulate. "What? I don't believe it."

"Believe it. Fired." She sighed. "It was a mistake to call you. I'm so mad, I can't even talk. I'll call you in the morning."

"That's too damn bad; we're going to talk, right now. You can't wake me up in the middle of the night, tell me we've been fired, and then say you don't want to talk about it. What the hell is going on?"

"That's exactly what I would like to know. Canfield would also like to have your answer to that question." Eileen was using her courtroom voice. "According to Stan, they have received serious complaints accusing you of imprudently conducting your investigation. Legal action against you, the firm, and the Canfield Insurance Company is also a very distinct possibility."

"What?" I squawked like a poorly trained parrot. "That's ridiculous."

Eileen ignored my screech. "Stan also received a report from Sheriff Price stating that the Dolphin Beach authorities do not believe Boyd was involved in Amanda's death. I've seen the report. Blaine, it appears to be legitimate. CIG is going to process the claim."

I tried to squeak out a weak response, but Eileen wouldn't listen. "I'm not finished. Canfied is planning to investigate. If they determine you acted injudiciously, they will terminate all dealings with our agency and initiate proceedings to have your license revoked."

I was stunned but relieved; Eileen had removed one nagging worry. During the last few days, I had been nervously looking over my shoulder, watching for another attack. My worrying had been a waste of energy; the nameless "they" found a more vulnerable point of attack. CIG yielded. I didn't want to think about the consequences, but Eileen proceeded to list them for me. I tried to ignore her.

"Well?" Eileen's voice brought me back. It was the tone which implied, "How the hell am I going to get you out of this mess?" A tone she had been using much too frequently lately.

"I need to think." I knew I should say more but couldn't think of anything.

A very unladylike snort rang in my ear. "It's a little late for you to start thinking. I want you to fly up here in the morning so we can plan our response to these allegations."

"No. Somebody in this town has gone to a lot of trouble to get me fired. I intend to find out who it is, and why."

"Goddammit! I have run out of patience with you. Your flight leaves at 8:00 A.M. You can fly back there later in the week and finish your vacation, I made the reservations; pick up your tickets at the airport. You can leave your car there for a few days."

"You better cancel them. And don't use that shitty big sister tone of voice because it won't work. I'm staying in Dolphin Beach until I figure out what's going on here. You can always go back to some fancy uptown law firm; I'm the one who's going to be out of work. Let me do this my way."

Click. Eileen hung up. This was getting to be a new annoying habit, one she learned from me. I sat on the edge of the bed, clutching the receiver. I almost turned on the light and dialed Eileen's number but didn't; she wouldn't answer. Tempers run in the family; it would be smarter to wait until she calmed down. With luck, it would only take two or three days—Eileen and I don't stay mad at each other longer than that.

"So much for fence mending." I hung up the phone and lay down. My mind churned with questions. Who had enough clout to scare off CIG? Could they get my license yanked? How mad would Eileen be when I didn't appear in the office tomorrow? We had survived worse battles; we would survive this one—I hoped.

I planned to sit up and worry, but my body wouldn't cooperate. Sleep was more important. I turned over on my stomach, punched the pillows, and was asleep before I could decipher the feeling of forgetting something important.

ON WEDNESDAY I woke a few minutes before the alarm sounded. I was stretching, looking at the rain when the telephone rang, ending an unenthusiastic attempt to convince myself to go outside for a run. I glared at the phone and toyed with the idea of yanking it out of the wall before it could deliver more unsettling news. But instead of following my instincts, I rolled over and grabbed the receiver.

"Ms. Stewart?"

I groaned and vowed to get rid of the telephone, as soon as I got rid of this caller. I did my best to sound wide awake. "Good morning, Sheriff Price. You're at work early this morning. What can I do for you?"

He chuckled. "We start early to keep ahead of the crooks. Hope I didn't wake you. Now I hear you ain't working for that insurance company anymore, but I thought you would like to hear our good news. You know, professional courtesy..."

Professional courtesy? I nearly laughed, but was afraid I hadn't heard the punch line yet.

"...We got a good line on the person who killed Mrs. Johnson."

"You've made an arrest?" Professional cynicism took over. I grabbed a pad from the nightstand and doodled while Price spoke.

"We found Mrs. Johnson's car, abandoned a few miles outside of town. It was loaded with finger-prints, hers and those of a punk named Wesley Seward. He's a mental case, been in trouble before. Car theft, burglary, stuff like that. He always got off 'cause he was a minor." The sheriff laughed. "Well, that asshole made a big mistake—he ain't a minor anymore and this ain't no petty crime."

"Do you have other proof? This doesn't sound like an airtight case."

"Now, don't you worry your pretty little head 'bout that. My men are pickin' him up right now. We'll get all the proof we need. Guess you'll be leaving soon to finish your vacation. Hope you enjoyed your stay in town."

Nice try; but I wasn't ready to leave. "It's not over yet. I may stay a little longer. What about Davis?"

He sighed. "We're still working on it. We found cocaine and other drugs in his locker. We may never learn who killed him but we do know his killing was drug related. It's upsetting to discover one of my men was mixed up in that dirty business. But that's no reason for you to hang around. We have your statement. We'll call if we need more information."

He uttered some platitudes; I listened and breathed a sigh of relief when he finally hung up. I wanted to think about Price's motives, but the phone rang again.

Shit, I'd never make it out of bed. Maybe when I got back to New York I could perfect the technique and conduct all my business over the bedside telephone, if I still had a business to return to after CIG finished its investigation. With that sobering thought in mind, I curtly answered the ringing monster.

A soft, vaguely familiar, male voice answered. "I'm sorry to call you so early; but it's urgent. This is Perry King. I need to see you."

I hesitated. I had more important things to do, things like saving my career—all my doubts about continuing to work had vanished during the night.

King hurriedly tried to convince me to meet him. "I can't go into specifics over the telephone—you'll have to trust me. It is important. Have you had breakfast yet?"

"It's only seven-thirty. I'm still trying to get out of bed. Perry, I don't have any free time today. Can we meet tomorrow?"

"No." He was insistent. "Let me buy you breakfast. I have to see you today—now. It concerns Amanda Johnson." He repeated his breakfast offer.

My curiosity was aroused and I was hungry. "Always eat breakfast," is one of the few rules of sensible living I faithfully adhere to. Not that I believe the nutritionists'—and mothers'—line about breakfast being the most important meal of the day. It's a simple fact of my life that breakfast is often the only meal of my day. I gave into King and my rumbling stomach. We made arrangements to meet in the hotel coffee shop.

THE RESTAURANT WAS crowded with tourists. King waved to me from a distant corner of the room. I wove through a crowd of slow-moving elderly people and slid into the booth. An ashtray, overflowing with crumpled, half-smoked butts sat in the center of the table, flanked by two thick ceramic mugs and a carafe of coffee.

King filled both cups and said, "I took the liberty of ordering for you; hope you don't mind. Thought I would treat you to a real Southern breakfast. It's the least I could do after dragging you out of bed so early in the morning."

A waitress emptied the overflowing ashtray and refilled the carafe. As soon as she was gone, King leaned back against the red vinyl cushions, lit another cigarette, and asked, "So, how's your client this morning?"

Showing admirable restraint, I declined the pack of cigarettes King held out and took a sip of coffee before answering, "My client is fine, thanks. Why do you ask?" And it was the truth. I had a brand new client: myself.

"That's not what I heard." He smiled. "Don't raise your eyebrows at me. This is a small town; news gets around fast. I heard you were fired. You don't have a client anymore."

Were these people tapping my phone lines? I took another sip of coffee and said, "Well, Perry, you heard wrong. My client is very satisfied with my work. Tell your gossipy friends that I'm still here, still working. And I'm not leaving."

"Good." The waitress reappeared and slapped platters loaded with eggs, ham, sausages, potatoes, grits and biscuits down on the table. The plates were barely visible under the load of food.

I cautiously stirred the grits, not sure I was adventurous enough to stick them in my mouth. Perry noticed and laughed. "You don't have to eat them. Lots of people don't like grits; don't know what they're missing." He ate the grits, and every other piece of food on his plate, with gusto.

There was a lot of untouched food on my plate; the eggs were dry, tasteless, and cold. The ham was cold and salty. I pushed the plate to the edge of the table and hoped the waitress would remove the dish. I grabbed a biscuit, took a bite, and reached for the jam. Maybe it would improve the taste. It didn't. Disgusted, I threw the biscuit on top of the pile of inedible eggs and poured another cup of coffee.

Perry scooped the last of the eggs from his plate and shoveled them into his mouth. I watched him attack the basket of biscuits, fascinated by his appetite. It was time to spoil his feast. "I have a busy schedule this morning. Why did you want to see me?"

"I was hoping the gossip was true and that you were looking for another client. I'd like to hire you."

"Why me? This town must have some competent people who can work for you."

"One of my clients was arrested this morning." His next sentence echoed my thoughts. "Nothing unusual about that; a lot of my clients manage to get themselves arrested. But this is different; the charge is murder. He's been charged with murdering Amanda Johnson—"

"Wesley Seward? He's one of your clients?"

King nodded, pushed aside his spotless plate, and leaned closer to me. "Wesley isn't capable of killing anyone. And I don't want to give the good citizens of this town any reason to close the Mission. They've tried before, using less serious charges. People here will pounce on us, accusing us of allowing murderers, rapists, robbers, and drug addicts to roam about unsupervised. This arrest will only substantiate their accusations."

He stopped to gauge my reaction, didn't see any, and went on to his closing argument. "And they will try to stop the shelter Amanda wanted us to build. We need your help; no one else in this town has enough courage to go up against the sheriff."

I listened with admiration; King was able to insert a lot of guilt-inducing statements into a few concise sentences. It didn't work; I resented his attempt to manipulate me and told him my feelings. "Thanks for the flattery, but I have a client. However, I do want to talk with Wesley. Where is he?"

"In jail. He was arrested shortly before I called you. Wesley used his one phone call to contact me—woke me up."

I smiled. "Happens a lot in this town. Does he have an attorney?"

"There's one on the Mission's board of trustees. I called her; she was going to police headquarters. You'll want to speak with her. She's expecting your call. Here's her card." He passed a business card across the table.

I looked at the card and read the name. "Katherine Lourdes. We've met." I drained the coffee cup and stuck my cigarettes into my purse. "I'll be in touch."

King grabbed my arm. "What are you going to do? Aren't you going to see Wesley? Shouldn't you . . ."

"Let me do my job. I know what I'm doing." How many times had I repeated that phrase during the past few days? I ignored that nagging question and left.

A vision of a large stopwatch floated into my mind, loudly ticking off the minutes until CIG managed to get my license revoked, or Eileen lost all patience with me. Or, I groaned—my conversation with Lourdes flashed into my head—Boyd found, and destroyed, Amanda's file.

ELEVEN

I MADE MY WAY back to my room to change clothes. I needed to run, think, and plan. My new friend Jim, who was always working, stopped me as I passed through the lobby. The package from my friends at the credit union had arrived. I signed for the overnight delivery and as I walked away, Jim said, "You have some other mail. If you can wait a minute, I'll get it."

Tick. Tick. Tick. The stopwatch was rapidly counting off the seconds. "No, don't bother. I don't have time. I'll pick it up later."

The credit report confirmed my snooping. Hollis Wilson, Certified Public Accountant, was having trouble paying his bills. "Slow Pay" and other collection agency euphemisms for people who ignore their bills were scattered across the report. A quick tally of the overdue balances made me, Queen of the Credit Card Junkies, shudder.

My submerged conscience made a long overdue appearance. If I started to suspect every American who couldn't afford to pay the bills, or was slow to pay, I'd have a list of a few million names. I stopped to light a cigarette, listened to the scolding voice inside my head, and started to burn the paper. A corner flamed before I changed my mind and extinguished the flame. I added the slightly charred report to my little horde—maybe it would be useful in the future.

The afternoon was wasted with interviews. Employees, ex-employees, business acquaintances, and friends; all repeated the same message: Amanda had been a wonderful person, great boss, an involved member of the community. She had a temper, but she worked at keeping it under control and always apologized for losing it. She expected honesty and hard work from her employees, and set the same high standards for herself. No one had any idea of who could be responsible for her death.

I lost count of the number of times I dialed Lourdes's office and was told, "I'm sorry. Miss Lourdes is still in court. Would you care to leave a message?" My predinner call was rewarded; Katherine answered, her voice tinged with exhaustion. "We just walked in. I expected to hear from you. Welsley's with me. I managed to get the judge to set bail and release Wesley in my custody."

"Your custody? Is that the usual procedure here?"

"It's a little unusual, but Wesley's...why don't you come to my office and meet him?"

THE SLIGHT YOUNG MAN on the leather sofa looked at me and suspiciously asked, "Are you a cop?"

"No. I'm a private investigator."

"Wow! A private eye!" He jumped up, grabbed my hand, enthusiastically pumped it, and flung questions at me. "You got a gun? Ever shoot anybody? Hey, do you know Magnum?"

The questions kept coming. I attempted to answer and pull my hand away.

"Wesley!" Katherine's voice whipped through his questions. "That's enough." He looked, dropped my hand, and slumped onto the couch.

"I'm sorry, I didn't mean nothing." He stared at the tips of his work boots and spoke bitter words. "I know my behavior was inappropriate. I can't help it—I'm just a dumb retard."

Lourdes shook her head and gently said, "Don't talk like that. You know it's not true. Why don't you go out to the kitchen and see if there's any pop in the refrigerator? Bring some back here for us too."

It took a long time for the attorney to shake a cigarette from the pack sitting on the desk and light it. I waited impatiently and finally said, "He's very upset." Lourdes lit a match and nodded in agreement. "Is he—"

"Retarded? Slightly. Capable of committing murder?" She tossed the match in the ashtray and shrugged. "Who knows? Given the proper conditions, or provocations, we're all capable of murder. Did Wesley murder Amanda?" She shrugged again. "I doubt it. Although Price is anxious to prove me wrong."

Wesley's hesitant steps in the hallway interrupted our discussion. He walked in, carefully balancing three glasses of soda on a silver tray. Three pairs of eyes remained focused on those tumblers as he took tiny, cautious steps across the room. The tray landed safely on the desk, accompanied by Wesley's sigh of relief and broad smile.

Lourdes distributed the glasses, looked at Wesley, and solemnly said, "Miss Stewart is going to help us. It's very important that you tell her the truth. Do you understand?" He mumbled an answer and shrank back against the leather cushions.

He was staring at his feet again.

I said, "Wesley?"

Without lifting his eyes from the floor, he said, "Yes, Miss Stewart?"

"Call me Blaine. You watch Magnum, right?" He nodded and started to answer. I cut him off and said, "Then you know how hard my job can be. And you can help. I'm going to ask you a few questions. Your job is to tell me the truth. Don't worry, I won't get mad as long as you tell me the truth."

Lourdes sat behind her desk, smoking her cigarette, impassively watching us. Wesley was chewing on a fingernail, apprehensively watching me. I said, "Wesley, remember, just tell me the truth. Did you—"

"No! No! No! I know what you're going to ask. I didn't kill Mrs. Johnson. I don't care what the sheriff says, I didn't do it! All I did was let Mrs. Johnson drive me home on Monday, nothing else. Why won't anybody believe me? Mrs. Johnson was my friend. I wouldn't hurt her."

"I believe you." I really did believe his pathetic outburst. "Tell me exactly what happened. Mrs. Johnson drove you home Monday night?"

"Yes, I work for her company. It's only a part-time job, but they gave me a uniform and I get to eat for free in the cafeteria—that's where I work, in the cafeteria. I keep the tables clean, throw away the garbage, and mop up the messes people make. Sometimes Mrs. Johnson drives me home, or to the Mission if I'm going there for a social."

"What time you leave on Monday?"

"That's easy." His face brightened; he was pleased to be able to answer. "I get off at three-thirty. That's cause I start at seven-thirty in the morning—got to help with the breakfast people. Mrs. Johnson came in for a cup of coffee just as I was finishing up and said, 'So Wesley, you want a ride?' I said 'Sure.' Then she said, 'Can you wait 'til I finish my coffee?' She always says that. When she was done, I helped carry her work out to the car. She says she likes to get home early to cook dinner for Mr. Johnson—she really likes to cook. And she can get more work done before Mr. Johnson gets home, and no one bothers her with phone calls. I really like her car. It can go real fast, but she never drives fast. She's a real good driver."

"So you left between three-thirty and four o'clock?" He nodded. "It wasn't any later than four?"

"No, ma'am, I was home by four o'clock. I got home in time to watch *People's Court* on TV. It's my favorite show. It comes on at four."

"Call me Blaine; it's easier. Do you live with your parents?"

"No Miss—Blaine." He smiled. "My parents are dead. I live alone."

Wesley proudly started to describe his one-room apartment. I held up a hand to stop the rush of words and asked, "What did you do Monday night after Mrs. Johnson drove you home?" His face was blank. I tried to explain. "Did you go out, go to the Mission? Did you see anyone, talk to anyone?"

"No, I...I watched televison. *The Wizard of Oz* was on. I didn't hurt Mrs. Johnson. Honest, I didn't hurt her." He sniffled, rubbed his eyes, and continued. "I don't know why Sheriff Price says I did. He doesn't believe me. I don't want to go to jail. The sheriff said I'll spend the rest of my life in jail; it don't matter how good Miss Lourdes is. He said she won't be able to get me off." Tears were openly flowing down his cheeks, he bowed his head, and tried to avoid our eyes, embarrassed to be crying in front of two women.

Did Price really believe Wesley had killed Amanda? I didn't know what evidence the police had gathered, but I would have a hard time believing it.

Katherine intervened. "Wesley, honey, calm down. There's no reason to cry. Remember, I said you shouldn't worry. Blaine is going to help us. We're a lot smarter than Sheriff Price. You're not going to jail." She continued talking in a soothing voice. Wesley stopped crying; a flicker of hope spread across his face.

I leaned against a bookcase, stuffed my hands into my pockets, and watched. Lourdes, finally satisfied that Wesley had recovered, sent him off to watch television.

Lourdes offered me a cigarette—one of those long, thin brown ones. I shook my head and said, "I don't want a cigarette; Katherine, you don't need my help, you need a judge with some sense."

"Price and a lot of others in this town think that Wesley, and anyone like him, is apt to go crazy and start raping and killing everyone in sight. These people think the 'retards' or 'crazies,' as they so delicately phrase it, shouldn't be allowed outside the grounds of an institution without an armed escort." She spat the words out. "'Crazy retard!' You don't know how many times I heard that obscene phrase today. I spent the day listening to Price's nonsense and trying to find a judge who agreed that Wesley's fingerprints in the car weren't sufficient evidence for a murder charge. Price wanted to keep that young man in jail without bail."

"Price told me Wesley has a record. What did he do?"

"Wesley got into trouble when he was fifteen. Price is trying to use it as an example of Wesley's degenerate nature. Wesley was in junior high school and started hanging out with a gang, trying to get accepted by the so-called normal kids. He went along for a joy ride and was abandoned by his friends, left to face the police alone. Wesley was put on probation. It turned out to be a good experience for him." She grinned and said, "If you'll excuse the expression, he was scared shitless."

"Has Wesley been in any other trouble?"

She shook her head. "No. Wesley's been a good tax-paying citizen of Dolphin Beach ever since. The juvenile records are sealed, but if Price runs true to form, it will be all over tomorrow's newspapers. The sheriff's department has some pretty big leaks; Price will be sure it gets out."

Lourdes walked to a cabinet near the window and selected a bottle. "Tomorrow is going to be an ugly day. People will be in an uproar, screaming about crazies and the dire threat the Mission presents to the community. You want a drink?"

Yes, I wanted a drink. My body ached for one. I could feel the warm glow of the alcohol sliding down my throat. I said, "No," and lit a brown cigarette from her pack, hoping it would ease the ache. I inhaled deeply and told myself it was better than drinking.

WHY WAS PRICE so anxious to charge Wesley? Why the smoke screen? I lay in bed and stared at the ceiling. My initial reaction was to pity Wesley. Upset by the death of his friend and boss and bewildered by the accusations made against him, Wesley had been only slightly cheered by our reassurance. The crestfallen, frightened expression had remained on his face as we said good night.

My pity transformed itself to anger. I rolled over and administered a violent punch to the pillows, wishing it was Price's face beneath my fists instead of goose down. In the daytime I had been too busy interviewing people to allow myself the luxury of the emotional outburst that keeps me sane when trapped in an insane situation. Now in the quiet, dark bedroom, all the suppressed emotions, the grief, the anger, and the fear flooded out. Tossing, turning, and punching the pillows didn't help; my frustration only increased until I jumped out of bed, pulled on some clothes, and went outside.

Insomnia was one familiar side effect of my job. Every sordid detail comes out at night, driving me from my bed to tramp the streets until exhaustion finally propels me back home for a few hours of disturbed, restless sleep. At least the beach would provide a pleasant spot for a late-night walk.

It wasn't a good idea. The beach was too quiet and deserted for my mood. I needed crowds and bright lights, not damp solitude. I headed for the brightly lit streets and found them empty. New York City had spoiled me. Unlike my usual city haunts, at one o'clock in the morning Dolphin Beach was dark and securely locked up. I walked past a bar, tightly shuttered boutiques, and one small restaurant that was still open, my fists jammed in the pockets of my windbreaker, thinking dark, evil thoughts.

A hand grabbed at my arm. I shook it off and whirled around. It was Hugh. Relief spread across my face (I would have to get over the habit of pulling a gun on him each time we met) as I relaxed.

"I was sitting in the coffee shop and saw you walk past. You didn't hear me calling. What are you doing out in the rain?" He pulled me under an awning and carefully looked at my face. "Are you okay?" He didn't need an answer; even in the dim light the exhaustion on my face was visible. "Come on." Hugh wrapped his arm around my shoulders. "I can't sleep either; it was a tough night in the emergency room. Let's walk for a while." We strolled in silence. After an hour of quiet walking, he looked down at me and asked, "Tired?" I nodded. We turned back to the hotel.

I WAS DRIFTING off to sleep when an image of the missing file flashed inside my closed eyelids. I sat up; Hugh stirred and said, "What's wrong? Where are you going?"

"I have to go out. There's some business I need to take care of." I pushed the sheet aside and started to get out of the bed, but Hugh grabbed my arm.

"It's four-thirty in the morning. You need to sleep, not worry about business. It will have to wait until tomorrow."

He was right; it was too late and I was too shaky with fatigue to attempt another break-in. I let him pull me down and fell asleep with my cheek resting against Hugh's shoulder. Four hours later I woke to find an empty bed and a note leaning against the bedside telephone. The note complained about a doctor's hours being worse than a private investigator's hours and ended with the question, "Why don't we both find normal jobs and live happily ever after?"

TWELVE

Thursday

THE RECEPTIONIST patiently repeated, "Mr. Johnson will be with you shortly. Please take a seat."

"Will you please try him again? I've been waiting for half an hour. I'm getting tired of waiting; I have other appointments."

"I'm sorry, Mr. Johnson said—"

"You told me what he said." The salespeople sitting in the lobby watched with amusement lighting their faces. Their curiosity didn't faze me. I raised my voice. "Will you check again?"

A security guard, not amused by our loud voices, strolled closer. He was not the infirm, semiretired type usually seen in stores, banks, and libraries. This one was young, alert, and muscle-bound.

The receptionist wasn't amused either. She looked past me and called out, "Clint, could you come here?"

Three long, powerful strides and he was standing beside the desk. "Something wrong, Mona?" Clint and Mona—I was too mad to smile at the two all-American kids, earnestly trying to do their jobs.

"This lady..."—Mona's voice vibrated with self-righteous indignation—"...keeps insisting that I allow her to barge into Mr. Johnson's office. She doesn't have an appointment. Mr. Johnson is in a meeting and can't be disturbed. He asked that she wait until he is free. She doesn't want to."

Clint glanced at me, disappointed by the simplicity of Mona's complaint. "Ma'am, we can't have you causing a disturbance. Why don't you have a seat and read a newspaper. Mr. Johnson will see you when he has the time."

"I am not causing a disturbance." I deliberately lowered my voice, clenching my fists until fingernails digging into my palms cautioned me to relax. "I've read the newspapers and all the magazines. I simply asked Mona to check with Mr. Johnson's office to get an idea of how much longer his meeting will run."

My brilliant smile worked. Clint turned to the receptionist and said, "Mona, why don't you ring Mr. Johnson's office and check with Jennifer? Maybe she can tell you how long he'll be tied up."

She smothered a curse and punched a three-digit extension number into the telephone console. Clint leaned against the counter, amused by the conflict. Mona spoke into the phone, listened, maliciously smiled at me, and handed the receiver to the guard.

"Yes, sir." He gave the receiver back to Mona and turned to me, the smile gone from his face. "I'm sorry; you'll have to leave the premises."

"What?" The curious faces from the lobby turned to watch. "You can't throw me out; I haven't done anything wrong."

"This is private property. We do whatever Mr. Johnson tells us. And he very clearly told me he didn't want to see you. He said you are not welcome on the grounds. If you don't leave, we will call the sheriff and press charges." An iron fist closed over my forearm. Clint's voice, and grip, were firm. "You have to leave."

Arguing was not an option. My choices were limited. I could try to fight my way into Boyd's inner sanctum or make a dignified retreat. I chose retreat, ignominiously escorted by the stern-faced Clint. He kept a tight grasp on my arm and allowed me to pause long enough to grab my briefcase. I stuffed an annual report into the leather case before the security guard dragged me to the exit. He ignored my snide, "Have a nice day," folded his arms across his chest, and stood in front of the building until I drove out of the parking lot.

The sun was bright and hot. I decided to take advantage of the respite from the storm and combine research with a picnic lunch by the waterfront. I stopped at a concession stand for a fish sandwich, found an empty table far away from the crowd, and opened the report. It was time to learn more about Amanda's business.

A corporation's annual report is often little more than an expanded commercial. This was no exception, hours of expensive marketing effort had gone into the preparation of this report. The glossy black cover featured a stark photo of the new BAJ personal computer—the BAJpc1000—softly glowing in the hidden backlighting. Simple white, block letters in the upper right corner of the cover proclaimed, BAJ

ENTERPRISES—1988 ANNUAL REPORT. Simple and elegant. The corporate image was eloquently delivered by one picture and five words.

I flipped through the pages and was subjected to glimpses of Amanda on every page. Posed shots of Amanda and Boyd proudly standing next to the prototype of their new computer; candid shots of Amanda working with her design team; formal portraits of Amanda, the President/Chief of Technical Development, addressing shareholders. Tears filled my eyes. I slammed the booklet closed, shakily lit a cigarette, and ordered myself to fight the tears. It worked—as it usually does. I reopened the report, prepared to be affected by only one emotion: curiosity.

The report was a slick advertising job, but the fancy prose couldn't hide corporate troubles. They jumped out at me from the first page. It began with a section labeled, "Corporate Profile." I rapidly scanned the paragraphs, circling a few items of interest.

"In 1988, BAJ Enterprises completed the expansion of its corporate universe. Terminals, monitors, printers, graphic displays, and keyboards—all meeting BAJ's high-quality standards—are now available to complement our software products. The initial reaction to our new lines has been favorable. Both the industry critics and the buying public agree; demand has significantly outpaced supply." Uh-oh, they can't build them fast enough.

"Due to construction delays, our new manufacturing facility in Taiwan did not become fully opera-

tional until mid-year. In addition, sporadic labor
disputes also delayed production. However, we are
very pleased to report to our shareholders that these
problems have been resolved. Our plant is operating
at maximum capacity; our labor unrest has been resolved..." I circled the paragraph, scrawled, "Back-
logs?" in the margin, and moved on.

Dealer network in place, selling contracts finalized
with two national chain stores and pending with three
other dealer networks. The optimistic tone turned
downbeat, "...a secondary stock offering, planned for
the last quarter of 1988, was postponed because of
adverse market conditions..." They planned to try
again in 1989. The paragraph ended with a plea for
stockholders to remain faithful and rally round the
company. Touching. I wondered if it had worked.

"BAJ Enterprises has entered the new fiscal year
firmly convinced of its ability to further solidify its
market share and achieve steady, profitable growth.
BAJ's considerable investment in its future and com-
mitment to the expanded product lines, growing dealer
network, state-of-the-art manufacturing complex,
while maintaining its leadership role in cutting-edge
software development, is beginning to pay off in increased sales...."

After several self-congratulatory sentences about
the healthy balance sheet, the writers returned to the
BAJ family theme. The final passage was intended to
bring tears to the eyes and investors to the stock.

"We are entering the new fiscal year with a profitable, growing company. But even more valuable than

any item on our balance sheet, is the BAJ family—the technical staff, the sales reps, the laborers in foreign lands, and all the support staff—our most important asset. Their contributions to this company cannot be measured. The past year was indeed troublesome for both our own company and the entire industry, but our family grew stronger in the face of adversity. Working together, we will continue on our path of increased growth to market leadership." The passage was signed, "Boyd F. Johnson, Chairman and Chief Executive Officer/Amanda M. Johnson, Ph.D., President/Chief of Technical Development."

Five pages of urbane journalese, five interesting points: not enough product, labour trouble, a stock issue no one wanted to buy, additional debt, wonderful people.

Swirling winds lifted the crumpled paper remains of my picnic from the table. I caught the wrappers and looked around. The park had emptied; lunch was over. Dark clouds were forming over the Atlantic, preparing to bring more rain. I gathered up the papers and left. It was time to prepare for the evening assault on BAJ Enterprises.

IF I HAD STOPPED berating myself for being careless, for not immediately searching for Amanda's missing file, and taken a few minutes to question my motives, I never would have left the hotel that evening. Instead of dressing in dark clothes, stuffing a flashlight, screwdriver, and other tools into one pocket, extra ammunition clips into the other pocket, and the pistol into its holster, I would have crawled into bed for an uninterrupted night of sleep and fled early the next morning, leaving Dolphin Beach to its corrupt inhabitants. Running away was not a solution. What was?

I fell back on an old excuse; thinking would have to wait. Soul-searching was a self-indulgent waste of time and energy. Denial and procrastination were excuses that had worked for the past two and a half years, why dump them now? I finished dressing and left.

I parked the car in a tiny strip mall a mile away from the BAJ building. Even though police patrols in the neighborhood were sporadic, I didn't want an extra-vigilant cop to spot my car near the darkened building and investigate. The mall's movie theater advertised a midnight showing of a horror classic; the lot was crowded with the cars of late-night film buffs, so mine shouldn't attract curious attention. I zipped up my sweatshirt, pulled the hood over my hair, and set off on a slow jog to the corporate park, trying to look like another exercise freak out for a midnight run.

The run calmed my nervous stomach and steadied my hands. The flimsy lock on the loading bay door didn't offer much resistance to my screwdriver. Popping locks is a specialty, a skill I learned from an old cop when I was on the New York police department. The lock opened, I slipped inside, and quickly pulled the metal door closed. One advantage of serving as BAJ's security consultant was that I knew the location of the alarms and the fastest way to override them.

Boyd's office occupied the north corner of the building. The door was unlocked; I made sure the drapes were securely closed before snapping on the flashlight. The thin beam of light shone on files on the desk top, but I didn't bother to look at them. People don't leave their personal files unguarded on top of the desk; those files are always hidden away.

I tested each drawer of the desk. The bottom was locked. Under normal circumstances, I could have easily opened the lock with ease. But these weren't normal circumstances; my picks were hundreds of miles away in New York. So I could shoot the lock open—a little extreme—or force it with the screwdriver or penknife. I chose the penknife, was unsuccessful, and brutally pried the drawer open with the screwdriver. The screwdriver slipped and gouged a deep cut in the hard wood. I wet my index finger and rubbed at the mark, trying to make it blend into the other scratches.

The drawer was filled with interesting papers: tax returns, spreadsheets, balance sheets, and personal correspondence. For a brief moment, I considered stuffing the entire contents of the drawer into the small daypack I carried, but it didn't take long for me to change my mind. Better to risk the noise of the copying machine than take the papers and hope Boyd wouldn't miss them.

I made the long, noisy trip to the copying machine three times, growing more nervous each time. With every brilliant flash of light from the machine, I flinched, expecting a tap of discovery on my shoulder.

None came. I laughed at my too-vivid imagination and returned to Boyd's office to examine my booty. Unless the weak flashlight was missing obscure details, the papers in my lap didn't reveal any vital secrets worthy of murder. There had to be more.

One more batch. I got to my feet and walked into the outer office for a last stand at the machine. What would I do if someone walked in while I was feeding Boyd's tax returns through the copier—wet my pants?

Wet my pants! I laughed; I knew where to find Amanda's file. I forced myself to finish the copying, carefully replaced the file, once again tried to rub out the deepest scratches, and checked to be sure I wasn't leaving any other trace of my visit before trotting down the hallway to Amanda's office.

Price was sloppy. The office wasn't locked; it wasn't sealed; it wasn't even roped off with police tape. My hunch was correct. I fished a tiny silver key out from beneath the paper clips, rubber bands, pencils, staples, and other garbage that collects in the top drawer of every desk in the world. The key unlocked the paper towel dispenser in the tiny bathroom in her office, as I knew it would.

Instinct had been fed by a timely flashback to college days. Amanda occupied her free time with exploring. Every inch of the campus was subject to her scrutiny. She always returned to our dorm room bursting with news of another exciting discovery. I rarely shared her enthusiasm.

Except on the day when Amanda recounted her discovery of a little-known rest room on the top floor of the student center. I listened with interest; this discovery could be useful. Elevator service was unreliable; few people had the energy to climb the four flights of stairs. Amanda had found the ideal hangout. We had a private office in the middle of the hectic student center.

She also discovered, and liberated, the keys to the paper towel dispenser. It became a receptacle for assignments, notes with the latest hot gossip, and occasionally, answers to exams. The janitor, happy for an excuse to bypass work, never disturbed our arrangement by trying to fill the holder with towels. Our little mailbox faithfully served us, without discovery, for the last two years of our college careers, holding messages of support, fear, encouragement, and hope. No one ever learned about our little cache.

The stainless steel box held a few paper towels, enough to keep the stiff cardboard envelope in place. I ripped the envelope open and found my message from Amanda, two micro diskettes from a personal computer. Amanda knew I would come across it—eventually. I stuffed the envelope into my pack. It was time to leave; I knew I wouldn't discover any more secrets.

THIRTEEN

Friday

IT WAS CLOSE TO four o'clock in the morning when I finally gave in to exhaustion, staggered into the bedroom, kicked off my sneakers, and collapsed on the bed. Undressing wasn't a major concern; it wasn't the first time I had slept in my clothes. The alarm clock, which I didn't remember setting, went off after a few hours and dragged me back to Dolphin Beach.

The urge to hit the snooze button almost won. I was telling myself another ten minutes of sleep would make me feel alert when the thought of the papers spread out on the desk jolted me out of bed. An icy blast of cold water from the shower head cleared just enough fuzziness from my brain to allow me to focus again.

I stepped out of the tub and pulled on a bathrobe. I shivered in the cold air—I had forgotten to turn the air conditioner to a lower setting before falling on the bed. I went to the desk to make my first call—it was time to call my broker.

Grace Hudson, Vice President, Garner Novill & Burnett, Members, New York Stock Exchange, answered on the second ring. It was seven forty-five, too early for her assistant to be in the office screening calls. "Blaine! Nice surprise. Early too." My inability to do anything before nine-thirty in the morning was well known. "You in the city? Thought you were on a long vacation."

"No, I wish I was in the city. I'm in Dolphin Beach—"

"Where?" Grace, a die-hard New York City native, refused to learn elementary geography—she simply refused to acknowledge the existence of other parts of the country. (Except, on rare occasions, California.)

"Don't worry. I'm still in the United States. But I didn't get up this early to give you a travelogue. I need advice." Grace waited, uncharacteristically patient. "This trip has turned into a working vacation. I've been looking into a company down here and the financial reports have gotten too complicated for me. Very early this morning, I realized I needed help from an expert. So I decided to call you before the market opened, before you got too busy to take my call."

Which was a lie—Grace always took my calls. We started out together almost ten years ago. She was a brand-new broker; I was a brand-new investor. During that time, we had both been successful in our endeavors; the friendship was an unexpected bonus.

"That important. The company?"

"BAJ Enterprises. They trade on the over-the-counter market—"

"Symbol?" Grace didn't waste time with complete sentences when a word or two would convey her message.

"BAJE. They—"

"Wait." I could hear her punching the letters into the terminal on the desk. "They closed yesterday at nineteen and a quarter. Been moving up the past few weeks." She punched a few more keys. "Anticipation of good earnings. Report will be out in a week or two. Stock dipped a few days ago." She was reading from the newswire, "Their president..." Grace's voice slowed but didn't show emotion. "Oh, I see why you're calling. Their president was murdered. The stock dipped and recovered. Blaine, I'm going to pull the annual report and the 10-K." The 10-K is another annual report companies are required to file with the Securities and Exchange Commission in Washington. "I'll read the reports. Talk to our analysts. Give me an hour."

Which gave me enough time for a quick run, to wake up completely, and a quick trip to the shopping mall. But first I had another call to make. Without hanging up, I dialed before I had time to think and lose my nerve.

The atmosphere was grim. Marcella didn't pass on any gossip; she immediately transferred my call to Eileen's office. Eileen didn't waste time with pleasant greetings. "I expected you yesterday." The angry inflection of her voice didn't surprise me; she was not accustomed to having her orders ignored.

"I told you I was staying here. A lot has been happening."

"A lot has been happening here too. I'm meeting with Stan Adams and CIG attorneys on Tuesday to discuss your behavior. I was hoping to have a little more to say than, 'Blaine was only doing her job.' You're not making it easy for me to defend you."

"Defend me?" My voice rose. I struggled to bring it down and change my approach; yelling at Eileen was never a good strategy. "Look, I'm sorry I didn't call you yesterday. I knew you were mad and thought I should give you some time to calm down."

"Yes, I was mad. I spent most of the day thinking. I couldn't sleep either." Not a good sign; Eileen was always able to sleep. I'm the one who suffers from insomnia. "I spent most of the night in the den, staring at the television." She took a deep, audible breath. "We can't continue this anymore. I want to dissolve the partnership."

Her words smashed into my solar plexus and left me breathless. I tried to answer but couldn't. Eileen was close to tears, but she managed to finish. "The past seven years have been great; working with you has been fantastic. No matter what was happening, I always knew I could rely on you. I trusted you. And now, I never know what you're going to do. I don't trust you anymore...." Her voice dwindled to a whisper and disappeared.

I gripped the telephone tighter, wanting to squeeze the misery out of her voice. "We can't do this over the phone. I need to see you; I'm going to catch the next flight to New York. I'll be there in a few hours."

"Don't bother. Don got back in town this afternoon. We haven't seen too much of each other lately; he's been flying a lot. I'm going home early; we're going to put the baby to bed, have a romantic dinner,

and leave early tomorrow morning for a long weekend at the shore. Just the three of us. Alone. No interruptions. Don's going to get reacquainted with his
daughter. I'm going to sleep late, take long walks on
the beach, and figure out what to do next.''

Eileen ignored my strangled protest and said, ''It's
too late for you to come rushing back; you had an
opportunity the other day and blew it. Finish whatever it is you're doing. I'll be back on Tuesday. Call
me: We need to make plans. Telling you over the telephone, without any warning, isn't fair, but continuing this way isn't fair either. I can't think of any other
solution.''

How could I answer? We turned into polite strangers, wished each other a good weekend and hung up.
Maybe I should have rushed home; maybe the outcome would have been different. But Eileen was right,
the only way out of this mess was to solve this case and
prove I wasn't crazy or unstable.

An urge to flee the room, the town, and the mess I
had made of my life struck. It almost overpowered my
resolve, but I forced myself to dress and gather up the
papers strewn across the desk, wanting to cry as I
stuffed everything into a manila envelope. ''Reality. I
chose reality,'' were the words I softly repeated. But
this was too much reality for me. I needed a drink. I
went out to the car and headed to the shopping mall.

THE BAJ PC1000 would be a hit with all of us high-tech
klutzes who are afraid to touch a computer. Putting
aside my misgivings, I followed the pictures in the

easy-to-understand manual and assembled the computer. Within half an hour of ripping open the first carton, I had empty boxes scattered across the floor and a new computer sitting on the desk, waiting to be plugged in. The ringing telephone interrupted my search for an outlet.

Grace sounded worried and began the conversation by asking, "What do you know about BAJ Enterprises?"

"Only what I read in the annual report. And a salesman just wasted half an hour trying to talk me out of buying their new computer. Too many problems. He said a cost-cutting campaign screwed up the quality; returns have been high. He also said the BAJ technicians were practicing cannibalism, stealing parts from one computer to fix another because the factory can't keep up with the demand. His store is considering dropping the BAJ line—it's too much trouble. What did you learn from your research?"

"The same. Rumors are flying. Everyone except the analysts and the people who buy the stock have heard them. Our company doesn't recommend the stock. Off the record, our analyst said, 'Keep the hell away from that stock.' Not good."

I asked a stupid question. "Do you have more than rumors?"

Grace never followed rumor; she always relied on fact. "Look at the balance sheet." I flipped open the well-thumbed annual report. "Look at the current assets, the accounts receivable, and the inventories..."

She patiently talked me through the report, giving me more detailed insights into BAJ's finances than I had been able to ascertain the previous evening. "...Those figures almost doubled between 1987 and 1988. Good indicator of too many returns, lack of quality control, improper screening of customers for credit-worthiness, overall poor management of vendors and suppliers."

Warming to the mysteries of the balance sheet, Grace launched into a technical discourse on current ratios, inventory turnover, and income statements. I broke into her monologue on earnings per share with a quick question, phrased in language Grace would respond to. "What's the bottom line?"

"BAJ is shaky. Management lost control over the product. Pumping out computers as fast as they can. Not concerned about quality."

"You said the stock has been going up in spite of the death of the company's president. Shouldn't this bad news have the opposite effect, force the price down?"

"BAJ worked hard to establish friendly ties with Wall Street. Earnings report due next week. People are anticipating a great report..."

The rest of Grace's sentence was lost in a flash of understanding. The significance of a memo from Boyd's office became clear. I hesitated and said, "I've seen that report."

"Wait—got to close the door." Grace dropped the telephone on the desk, and I heard the faint bang of a door being slammed. She came back on the line. "Positive it's the first quarter's earnings report?"

"Yes." During the time it took Grace to walk across her office, shut the door, and return to the phone, I had ripped the envelope open and scanned the report. It was clearly marked with a date—next Friday's date. "I have a copy right here in front of me."

Grace was startled into complete sentences. "Don't tell me how you got it or even hint at what it says. And don't even think of putting in any orders on that stock; the government frowns on insider trading and I like my job too much to start a new career. Blaine, I'm not sure what you're getting involved in but I have two bits of advice. Watch yourself and call if you need more information."

THE COMPUTER was waiting. I plugged it in and flipped the switches to turn on the computer and monitor. I was rewarded with a blank screen. Now what?

I consulted the manual, then slipped Amanda's disk into the proper slot and switched to the proper drive. Back to the manual for more instructions. I typed "A:" and hit the enter key. The computer blipped. My self-congratulations ended when I read the message that appeared: ENTER PASSWORD. I threw the useless manual to the floor and stared at the blinking cursor.

Password? I tried every combination of name, initials, telephone numbers, birthdates I could remember. None of my attempts succeeded. Each entry was greeted by another obnoxious beep and the words, "Invalid password. Enter your password now."

Something from college? Dorm room numbers, date of graduation. Nothing worked. The offensive tone and polite invitation to try again answered each attempt. I closed my eyes and rested my forehead against the terminal, trying to draw inspiration from long-buried memories.

Frustration stirred and brought back remembrances of my first encounter with computers and Amanda. Amanda was not the most patient tutor. She'd watch my struggle with data entry cards and printouts, and ultimately lose her temper as I fought to master the technological monster that had forced me to seek her tutelage. The keyboard, printout, or other offensive material would be yanked from my hands. She would snap, "Now pay attention. I'll show you how it's done in the real world. You're so spastic," and instantly correct the problem.

I smiled—I knew the password—opened my eyes, and typed SPAZ—my computer room nickname, bestowed on me by my impatient coach. The screen went blank, then a short paragraph appeared on the monitor:

Dear Spaz:
I'm glad you didn't forget too much. Congratulations on getting this far. I knew you would. The rest is easy. [Amanda had always been a master at uttering naive, optimistic understatements.] Maybe I'm being paranoid, but I've been trained to back up all my systems. If you are reading this,

it means we haven't had a chance to talk and I'm probably in trouble.

I wiped my eyes with the back of my hand and continued.

I've stumbled across some troubling information and want you to investigate. This disk contains an outline of what I've learned during the past week or two. I don't have many real facts and figures, just a lot of suspicions. But you're the detective—the rest is up to you.

Page after page, I alternated between being amazed and horrified by Amanda's epistle. I rapidly scanned the information, anxious to learn everything Amanda had discovered before her death.

The last page contained another short note from Amanda:

So Spaz, still with me? I hope none of the above is true. I hope you decide I've been working too hard and need a long vacation far away from computers. Whatever you do, be careful. It's impossible to distinguish the good guys from the bad. Don't trust anyone. But then, as I said before, you're the detective...

The familiar, frustrating sound of an incoming telephone call rang through the suite. Maybe it was Eileen, calling to retract everything she'd said during our earlier conversation. I snatched it, eager to hear her voice, anxious to solicit her advice.

A deep baritone voice shattered my hopes. It was Hugh. "I know it's early, but I wanted to talk to you before you left." He sensed my disappointment and said, "Are you busy? I can call later."

I said no, and he went on. "How about dinner tonight? I'm going to be substituting at the hospital this weekend so if tonight isn't good, we won't be able to see each other until Monday or Tuesday."

My first impulse was to decline, but because I was afraid to face a solitary evening, and the increasingly strong urge to drink to numbness, I accepted. We made arrangements to meet at the Piney Inn and hung up. I turned back to the computer to make notes and compare figures before reaching for the telephone.

Grace kept me on hold for a minute before picking up my call. "Door's already closed. What's up?"

"I have a question about a hypothetical situation. Suppose you were looking into a company and discovered they had two different sets of balance sheets and earning statements. They didn't like the original one, so they made up better figures for the second version. The second version looked so good, the company sent it out to the analysts and anyone else who was interested in buying the stock. What would happen to the company and the people who sent out the phony reports?"

Grace didn't ask questions I couldn't or wouldn't answer. She asked, "How did they fake the reports?"

"Company computers were rigged so returned products weren't recorded on the books. The reports they released show a return of one out of every thirty machines shipped. In reality, one out of every three computers has been returned. Sales figures for last year and the first quarter of this year were also inflated. They did a little more than round up to the nearest dollar. It looks as if sales were inflated by nine or ten million dollars."

"Proof?"

"I'm working on it. The CEO won't let me inside the building. He's annoyed with me at the moment. But I do have a lot of accusations." A dead woman's charges, I didn't mention that.

"Falsifying financial records. No one in this fictitious company is going to see you. Why is the CEO mad at you?" Grace ticked off excellent reasons for Boyd to keep the deception hidden. "Criminal charges: mail fraud, security fraud, and conspiracy to commit fraud. Civil charges: Investors will want their losses reimbursed. Maximum sentence: five years in jail, two hundred fifty thousand dollar fine, restitution to the fraud victims?"

"What would happen to the stock if the public learned about this?"

"Last year a company in Ohio had a similar problem. Stock fell 60 percent on the day the news became public."

"What proof would the authorities need in a case like this, assuming this actually happened? Who are the authorities?"

"Blaine, cut out this theoretical bullshit. This is BAJ." I started to answer but she stopped me. "You're in over your head. I'll make some calls and get you in touch with the right people. Damn, it's almost five-thirty; everyone's gone for the weekend. Maybe I can do something but don't expect results until Monday. I'll call you. Sit tight. Don't do anything."

Good advice. So, it wouldn't be the first time I didn't follow Grace's advice.

FOURTEEN

I STOPPED AT THE top of the post office stairs, looked at my watch, and cursed. Price was at the curb leaning against my car, his right hand casually resting on his pistol. Hugh would have to be patient; I was going to be late.

The sheriff tipped his hat. "Good evening." I politely returned the greeting and waited at the bottom of the stairs.

"I was admiring your fancy car. Sorry to see it isn't filled with suitcases." He acknowledged the grimace on my face. "Now don't you give me one of your sassy looks. Your work here is done; you don't have any business hanging around Dolphin Beach any longer. I'm telling you to pack up and get the hell out of here."

"Does the Chamber of Commerce know you're in the habit of ordering people to leave town? That approach can't be too popular with the tourists."

Sweat was rolling down his face. Price swiped at his forehead with a large red bandanna and stuffed the cloth into his back pocket before answering, "Ordinary tourists don't spend their evenings at the Docks buying drugs."

"Your spies are giving inaccurate reports. I wasn't buying drugs, although it wouldn't have been diffi-

cult; you should spend more time threatening drug
dealers and less time threatening me.''

Price stared at me. His mirrored sunglasses reflected my unconcerned face. My acting abilities held
steady; I calmly looked into the glasses without blinking. The sheriff spat into the street, narrowly missing
my feet, and said, ''You better spend less time worrying about my business and more time worrying
about your ass. Either get out of here or keep looking
over your shoulder, some mighty nasty people might
be following.''

I laughed. ''I'll be sure to ask for police protection.
Now, will you please get off my car, I'm late for dinner.''

Price stepped back from the car and started to issue ''one last piece of advice—''

I slammed the door and missed Price's last bit of
wisdom. He walked to his patrol car and climbed into
it. I drove away; several nervous checks in the rear-
view mirror confirmed the crawling feeling on the
back of my neck—the police car was following. The
blue-and-white patrol car stayed with me until we
reached the sign proclaiming the end of the Dolphin
Beach city limits where the car made a wide, slow turn
and drove back to the town.

''YOU SEEM PREOCCUPIED.'' Hugh tried to keep irri-
tation out of his voice. Dinner was almost over and I
couldn't even remember what had been served.
Hugh's attempts to be a perfect dinner companion
were wasted; I was too busy worrying about Price's

most recent intimidation attempt, Eileen's ultimatum, and everything else to pay attention.

I pushed the plate with the remains of my half-eaten meal to the side of the table and tried to apologize. "I'm not very good company."

He nodded. "You're right. Do you want to talk about it? I can't give you a back rub but I can listen, maybe even offer some good advice."

I scrutinized his face, trying to decide if I could trust him. I needed someone to listen as I thought out loud, worked out my strategy. My eyes misted; listening and offering opinions was a role Eileen usually assumed. I lit a cigarette and said, "Maybe I do need to talk..." and began an edited version of the past two days' activities.

Hugh's plate joined mine at the side of the table. He stopped eating and focused all his attention on my story. When I finished recounting my tale, he took a sip of wine, and asked, "Do you think Boyd killed Amanda for the insurance money?"

I speared a piece of fried grouper from my plate and thoughtfully chewed the cold fish. "It's been done before." I waved the empty fork in the air. "But I don't think he killed her. I've seen guys like him before; fraud is okay but murder is taboo. Boyd's too smart to have killed Amanda; he needed her to keep the company from going under. Remember, she was the technical genius; Boyd is going to have a difficult time replacing her. No, he didn't kill her."

Hugh put his fork down on the table and asked, "So who's your prime suspect?"

"I'm not sure yet. After listening to Price's not too subtle threats, I'm positive Amanda stumbled onto some important information about the drug trade down here and that the sheriff is involved. I need to find this Jessica; she could fill in a few of the blanks."

Hugh precisely arranged the silverware in a straight line before asking the question that was bothering him. "Price gave you a clear warning against getting involved?"

"Yes." I shrugged.

"Have you stopped to think that if Price is entangled in this drug trade, you could find yourself in a very dangerous position?"

"Yes." Thought about it? It was keeping me awake at night. I shrugged once again and—with more conviction than I felt—said, "What can I say? I'll take reasonable precautions but I'm not going to scurry away because Price is making threatening noises. He's not going to stop me."

Hugh frowned. "I'm worried, even if you aren't. What are you going to do next?"

It was time to change the subject, find less controversial ground. I smiled and said, "Have dessert?"

Hugh exploded. "What the hell are you trying to prove? You're not Superwoman. Get some help!"

I watched the bubbles rise to the top of my glass of seltzer and burst. "I would love to call in the reinforcements and let them take over. But I can't do that, not yet. Who should I call? And what am I going to say? I don't have any proof just a lot of wild accusations. Believe me, Hugh, as soon as I can substantiate my theories, I will call everyone who can possibly help and invite them to join me. I don't have the slightest desire to become a dead hero.''

"Then leave it alone. You've done enough. Let some agency take over.''

"How can you make such a ridiculous suggestion?'' Several heads turned to look at us. I took a sip of the seltzer and stared at the tablecloth until they lost interest and turned back to their meals.

Hugh frowned. ''Amanda is dead. Davis is dead. I don't want to see you dead. File a report with somebody who will be interested enough to follow up and get out of this mess before—''

"Forget it!'' The heads swiveled back to the action at our table. I didn't care. ''It's been too easy for me to walk away from my problems, too easy for me to say, 'Someone else will take care of it.' Sorry, Hugh, but this is my problem and I'm not going to walk away. If I give up because Price made some wild threats, the vision of Amanda's bloody face and the rain streaming down that copper coffin will haunt me forever. I have too many ghosts haunting me now; I'm not going to permit Amanda to join them.''

Hugh shook his head. ''I don't understand. One day you tell me you're going to quit; tonight you jump down my throat because I have the audacity to suggest that you follow your instincts and quit.'' He shook his head and was interrupted by a rude beeping noise from his jacket pocket. ''Damn, that's the hospital. Excuse me.'' He stood up, threw the linen napkin on the seat, and stalked off to find a telephone.

I watched Hugh walk away and wondered if he was right, but I knew I couldn't quit. A light touch on my arm broke into my thoughts. I jumped, it was Hugh. "Sorry, I didn't mean to startle you. I have to go. There's an emergency at the hospital." I started to pick up my purse, but he stopped me. "No reason for you to leave. You have your car; stay and finish your coffee." He laughed. "Have dessert. I'll call you tomorrow."

He grabbed his suit jacket and turned to leave. I called out, "Wait—stop by the inn when you're finished."

"I might be late..."

"Don't worry about the time; I haven't been sleeping much lately." I gave him a sly smile. "You'll probably need a nightcap, or a massage."

"Okay." He answered with the wide grin I found so attractive. "I'll be there."

Seconds after Hugh disappeared, an elderly waitress hurried to the table. "More coffee, Miss?" She refilled the cup. "Dr. Hugh, that's what I call him, told me to take good care of you. He said, 'Lucy'— that's me—'take good care of my lady friend. See that she gets whatever she wants. Put it on my tab,' he says. 'I'll take care of it next time I see you.' I've been waiting on Dr. Hugh since he was a little one. His parents, lovely people his parents, used to bring him here for Sunday dinner. They'd come here as soon as the preacher let them out of the morning service." She looked around and whispered, "His daddy liked his liquor. Never got drunk, mind you, but Lordy, he sure did like his drink.''

Lucy chattered away; my intermittent smiles and nods encouraging her to continue. She rambled deeper and deeper into the past; her words became a faint buzz in my ears, accompanying my thoughts which were firmly rooted in the present. A tiny piece of her story broke through my reverie, I looked up and interrupted her, ''What did you say?''

She blinked, flustered by my rudeness. Her Southern accent grew more pronounced. ''Lordy miss, I don't know.'' She giggled. ''I wasn't paying much attention.''

''The Docks—what did you say about the Docks?''

My intensity frightened her. Lucy pondered and slowly tried to answer, anxious to please. ''Lordy, let me see if I can remember. I was saying how Dr. Hugh loved to go out with Jack, my late husband—may he rest in peace—on Jack's fishing boat...''

''No, not that part.'' I tried to restrain my excitement. ''What did you say about the piers?''

''The piers. Lordy, that's easy.'' A smile lit her creased face. ''Dr. Hugh was always so excited about going out with Jack that he would stay up all night, waiting until dawn when the tide would be high enough for the fishing boats to get out...''

And high enough for the drug boats to get in. ''Where can I find a tide chart? I need to find out when high tide will be tomorrow morning.''

''Honey, you want to go fishing? Lordy, you had me worried, asking questions so hard and so fast.

That's an easy one. Jack's been dead six years now, God rest his soul, but I still check the tide charts every day. Tide will be high at 6:47 A.M." She smiled and waited for another question.

I resisted the impulse to shout "Lordy!" and said, "I could kiss you. You've solved my problem." I grabbed my purse and hurried to the parking lot. Six forty-seven A.M. I had to prepare for my meeting with Jessica.

Lucy watched me, mumbled, "Lordy, Lordy," and began to clear the table.

FIFTEEN

I GLANCED AT the mirror: The headlights were still there—as they had been for the past few miles. The road ahead was dry and deserted; the driver didn't have any reason to dawdle behind, a few feet from my bumper. I moved closer to the shoulder to give him, or her, a clear view and plenty of room to pass. He didn't take the hint. The headlights moved closer.

The glare from the bright lights was annoying; a faint throbbing started behind my eyes. I adjusted the mirror so the light wasn't reflecting in my face and was struck by a flash of apprehension. I gently pressed on the accelerator; my uninvited guest easily kept up. My anxiety deepened, that car was purposely following.

We slid around a sharp curve at sixty miles an hour into a long stretch of ruler-straight blacktop. I jammed the gas pedal to the floor, attempting to outrun my pursuer. It didn't work; the car behind stayed close. The speedometer nudged ninety, wavered, and moved past to ninety-five, then one hundred, and kept moving. Both cars hurled through the inky darkness in a tunnel of empty fields and dark pine trees, headlights occasionally catching the red glow of the eyes of an animal sitting by the roadside watching our swift, quiet parade.

My mind rapidly clicked off options; there weren't many. If the other driver remained content simply to follow, I was confident I'd be able to find my way back to town and the safety of people without difficulty. A nagging voice reminded me that in this case "if" was a pretty big word.

My eyes never blinked; all my energy was focused on the road ahead. We passed through an intersection and into another banked curve. I found the line racing drivers always seek and floated through the turn without losing any speed.

I came out of the curve and smashed my foot down on the brake. The road was blocked by a car angled across it; a blue light on the roof of the car slowly revolved, illuminating two policemen standing beside it, guns in hand. It was not a comforting sight.

The tailing car pulled up and parked inches from my fender, effectively blocking any chance for retreat. I lowered the window, turned the engine off, and waited, my hands resting on the steering wheel, clearly visible to the approaching men—I didn't want to give them any reason to use those guns.

One man walked to the passenger side of the car; I was acutely, and uncomfortably, aware of the gun he pointed at me. The other cop walked to the open window, shone a powerful flashlight on my face, and said, "Let me see your license."

I ducked away from the glare and tried to sound confident. "What's going on here? I didn't do anything wrong; that car was chasing me."

The beam followed my movement; the cop ignored my protest. "I said I want your license."

"Okay, okay. It's in my wallet. Tell your buddy over there that I'm reaching into my purse for my wallet, nothing else—I don't want to get blown away by a nervous rookie." I handed the plastic-coated card through the window and sat back, thinking furiously as he studied the document. This wasn't a routine stop for a traffic violation; I knew the situation would only get worse. But all I could do was wait, watch for an opening, and try to regain control.

The man compared my face with the picture on the license, grunted with satisfaction, and slipped the paper into a breast pocket. He opened the car door and said, "Get out. Slowly. Face the car and put your hands on the roof."

I looked at the pistol in his hand and quietly followed his instructions. I know when to argue and when to shut up.

A bearlike figure left the car behind mine and ambled over to join the two cops. I watched, curious to see the driver's face. The man was huge, at least six and a half feet tall and 275 pounds heavy—muscle, not fat. My heart skipped a beat; he was also dressed in a sheriff's department uniform.

Too many cops—I was beginning to feel alone, abandoned, and set up. My mind veered off to dangerous thoughts: this roadblock was too easy, Hugh's emergency too convenient. Could Hugh be involved? I didn't want to believe it but . . .

I had been too willing to dismiss his timely arrival on the scene as coincidence: too willing to trust him, accept him. I shut my mind off; this wasn't the time to question my judgment, rattle my confidence, doubt my instincts. These questions, I told myself could definitely wait until later. Procrastination could be healthy.

The grizzly bear took charge; he quickly gave orders that the other men followed without question. "Bobby, you keep that gun ready. Luke, make sure she ain't carrying anything."

Luke's search was rough but it didn't have to be thorough. He quickly found the automatic, yanked it from the holster, and passed it back to the bear, who looked at it and said, "Nice, custom job. Thanks, honey, think I'll hang onto this for a little while."

I felt a bubble of anger inside my chest and pushed it down, afraid the anger would transform itself into uncontrollable panic. Without turning around I said, "That gun's legal; I have a license for it. Will you please tell me what the problem is here?"

Someone said, "Shut up." I heard the faint clank of metal against metal, and a cold, stainless steel band closed around my right wrist. Before I could react, both hands were jerked from the car roof and pulled behind my back. The other ring of the handcuffs tightly locked around my left wrist.

The men ignored me; I took a deep breath to steady myself and turned to them. The big man glanced at me and, before I could say anything, said, "Shut up."

I missed the warning inflection in his voice and said, "Don't tell me to—" A beefy hand darted out and raked across my face. I rocked against the car, recovered, and took a step forward. The revolving light on the roof of the police car painted our faces with a sickly bluish tint; no one else moved, no one spoke. He smiled. "Come on, honey, you got something else to say?" The man's fist hovered in the air, daring me to speak. I chose to ignore the taunt and remained silent, defiantly staring into the glittering eyes.

One of the other cops, Luke, intervened. "Dave, cut it out." He nervously looked down the road. "Let's get the hell out of here before somebody comes along and sees us. You take her. Bobby and I'll go back to town and dump her car at the hotel."

Dave's eyes burned into mine; the fist slowly moved away from my face and down to his side. A menacing grin stretched the corners of his mouth; his hand easily wrapped around my forearm. He whispered, "Okay honey, let's go. We'll have plenty of time to finish this later."

We stood on the side of the road and watched the taillights of the cars disappear around a curve. I shivered and for the first time in my life understood the cliché of breaking into a cold sweat—I could feel it trickle down my back. Pulling against the handcuffs would be a waste of energy, but I tried anyway. They held.

Dave opened the back door of his patrol car and roughly pushed me inside. He got into the front and started the engine; the click of the doors locking echoed through the car. I shivered again and concentrated on watching the roadside. There weren't any landmarks to note, only low scrub pine trees broken by empty fields. Through the breaks in the trees I caught glimpses of moonlight shining on the bay beyond the fields, the distance growing smaller and smaller as we neared the end of the peninsula.

A barrier marked the end of the blacktop; the sandy beach and harbor lay past it. Dave swung the car off the pavement into a small gap between the trees. Our destination was no longer a secret; the flash of the lighthouse beacon grew more intense as we neared the white finger of brick marking the harbor entrance.

The car bumped off the asphalt and landed on the soft, sandy trail. Too narrow to be called a road, the opening was barely wide enough for the car to pass. Pine trees grudgingly gave way, their branches slapping against the car, screeching against the metal like fingernails dragged across a blackboard.

I shuddered, remembering the sound from the evening when I maneuvered the Porsche down a similar track to view Amanda's body, and tried to avoid thinking about what might happen at the end of this path. Fear mixed with my memory of Amanda's bruised face; a vision of her body, with my face superimposed on it, flashed before my eyes. I moaned softly—I didn't want to be the next body dumped in a swamp, uncovered by a dog on its evening run.

Panic threatened to engulf me; a scream built inside my chest. If I opened my mouth, the shriek would roar out, bouncing through the quiet car. I took a deep breath—and let it out slowly, quietly. Jeff's voice came to me, "If you're going to win, you've got to stay calm. The biggest mistake you can make is to panic and stop thinking about a way out. Just stay cool and wait for an opening; you'll be all right." The terror subsided as quickly as it had come.

My struggle had not passed unnoticed. Dave laughed. "Don't be nervous, honey, we're almost there. You and I are going to spend some time together." When I didn't answer, he laughed again and said, "Don't feel like talking? Just wait, honey, soon you'll be begging to talk."

The car stopped in front of a shack at the base of the lighthouse, the same lighthouse Hugh had pointed out during our ill-fated walk on the beach. It was hard to believe that episode had occurred only a few days ago. A solitary police car was parked in the field outside the cabin; I took a deep breath, not out of fear but in preparation for facing whatever, or whoever, waited inside.

We parked behind the other car. Dave shut off the engine and turned to me. "We're here, babe. It's show time." I didn't want to go inside that cabin but didn't have any choice. He opened the door and dragged me out of the car and up the cabin stairs. My struggling was useless; he was too strong and without the use of my hands I couldn't break away.

The screen door was propped open, the cabin's inhabitants hoping to catch a stray ocean breeze. Their hopes were in vain; any breeze was efficiently blocked by the sand dunes rising at the edge of the field of sea

oats. Dave, annoyed by my squirming, announced our
arrival by giving me a sharp jab in the back and saying, "Here's your little hellcat. Man, she sure has been
trying to put up a fight."

Dave's hand pushed me off balance. I struggled to
stay on my feet; a rough hand caught my shoulder and
forced me down onto a hard, metal chair.

The hand was attached to Sheriff Price. I wasn't
surprised. I only wished there had been an easier way
to confirm my suspicions. Our eyes met but we didn't
speak—my mouth was too dry and Price was busy
talking with my escort, making sure his instructions
had been followed.

The Light House Commission had not provided the
Dolphin Beach Light Station keeper with fancy ac-
commodations; we were in a sparsely furnished, one-
room shack. The kitchen—a two-burner stove, sink,
and battered refrigerator—occupied one cramped
corner of the room. The furniture consisted of a
rocking chair placed in front of a dirty fireplace and
the battered table next to me.

The table, its Formica top marred with scratches
and cigarette burns, was littered with fishing tackle, a
scale, and several plastic bags filled with white powder. The small bags were marked. I leaned closer to
read the labels. LIGHTNING—underlined by a jagged
thunderbolt—another ugly suspicion confirmed.

A dull, aching pain was speading through my
shoulders and wrists, settling in the center of my chest;
I shifted to find a more comfortable position, but the
movement only sharpened the throbbing. Price no-

ticed my frown of discomfort and laughed. "Dave, I do believe your guest isn't very comfortable." He smiled and said to me, "We've been remiss, ignoring you. Please excuse our bad manners."

"Don't you worry, sheriff. I am truly enjoying your warm Southern hospitality. Nice little shop you have here—is this where you killed Amanda?"

I instantly regretted those words. Price raised his hand and struck my face with his open palm. "You think you got it all figured out, don't you? Well, you're not as smart as you think. Amanda Johnson was warned 'bout meddling; so were you. Too bad y'all didn't listen."

The gold edge of his college ring tore across a corner of my mouth. A drop of blood rolled down my chin and splashed onto my blouse. I watched the stain spread on the white silk and irrationally thought of the scolding I would receive from my dry cleaner. I smiled.

Price was enraged. He yelled, "You stupid bitch! You think this is funny? Ain't nothing funny 'bout the trouble you caused me." He raised his hand; I ducked, knowing I wouldn't be able to take too much of a pounding. My evasive movement satisfied Price; he interpreted it as fear and withdrew his hand. "Okay, now you listen carefully. I ain't in a mood to fool around. Boyd Johnson reported a burglary. Somebody broke into his office last night and wasn't too careful about it. Broke into his dead wife's office too."

I didn't try to answer—what could I say? Price's voice grew solemn. "Amanda Johnson had some papers that belonged to me. I've got an eyewitness who saw you about a mile away from that building; I think you ran off with those papers. I want them."

Stalemate. We stared at each other. I remembered the advice given during a college lecture on self-defense: "Whatever you do, don't make the situation worse." I waited; whatever I said would make things worse.

Dave, who had been leaning against the wall smoking a cigarette, flipped the spent butt through the door and took a step closer to us, his eyes bright with excitement. "Sheriff, let me try. She'll talk for me."

Price told him to calm down and turned back to me. "Dave gets a little crazy at times, specially if he starts playing around with his knife. You're a smart lady; I'm sure we can talk without Dave's assistance. You know you will eventually, so why put yourself through a lot of misery?"

Good question. Price wasn't interested in my answer; he had more important concerns. "I had your hotel rooms searched earlier this evening."

"That doesn't surprise me. I've been expecting it ever since a dead rat found its way inside. Was that your idea?"

The Sheriff nodded. "Dave took care of it personally—he is handy with that knife, don't you think?"

I looked over at Dave, who was back leaning against the door frame waiting for his time to play, and thought of the rat's slit throat. My stomach jumped. He smiled at me and with studied casualness, unsnapped a sheath attached to his gun belt, and slipped a folded hunting knife into his hand. My heart started to pound; the intimidation attempt was going to work—if I let it. I wrenched my eyes back to Price, shrugged, and said, "I wasn't too impressed."

"Stop the bullshit. Your suite was clean. Where are those papers?"

"The papers that describe your cocaine business, tally your income, and list your investments?" I shook my head. "Sorry, I don't know anything about them."

"Stupid bitch." The sheriff's hand darted out and slapped across my face. The force of the blow pushed me against the back of the chair; I winced as a wave of pain vibrated through my arms and shoulders. "I ain't gonna ask again. What did you do with the files you stole?"

The self-defense courses never gave a hint about what to do when the situation thundered out of control, an avalanche roaring down the mountainside. Maybe, in an extreme situation, the opposite approach would work—it had before. I stared into Price's eyes and said, "Fuck you."

A slow flush of anger spread over the sheriff's face. He stepped back. "Okay. You had your chance." He walked behind the chair and said, "Dave, have fun."

An expectant smile danced across Dave's face; he slowly straightened up. The knife blade snapped open. My eyes fixed themselves on the stainless steel cutting edge as it glided closer and closer to my throat.

Price's soft voice floated over my shoulder. "The files; where are they?" I didn't answer. The point of the knife pressed into the hollow at the base of my throat. I didn't flinch, didn't move.

The pressure increased. "Answer the sheriff's question."

I'd never been in a position like this before—no backup, no one knew where I was, no hope of help arriving. Hell, I couldn't even defend myself. I was afraid to think because it was impossible to visualize an outcome that didn't involve bloodshed or death; thinking would have resulted in an admission that the situation was hopeless and out of control. But I wasn't ready to concede defeat; I wet my lips and said, "Why don't you put that knife away and stop trying to scare me. It's not working. I don't have any damn files."

The knife deftly slid down to the top button of my V-necked blouse; tiny, crimson beads of blood oozed from the cut. Dave waited for my reaction, a satisfied grin on his face. I looked down at the thin, red line and said, "You're wasting your time fooling with drugs— you should have been a fucking surgeon."

The knife clattered to the floor. Iron fingers closed around my neck and lifted me from the chair. The hands squeezed harder and harder; the only sounds were my frenzied gasps for air. Powerless without the use of my hands, I helplessly twisted in his grasp; my weak struggling encouraged Dave to tighten his grip.

I started to black out. With detached curiosity, but no fear, I thought, "This is it, this is how I'm going to die."

Price yelled, "That's enough!" The hand relaxed but didn't leave my throat until Price pulled them away.

I dropped to my knees, bent double, coughing and fighting for air. Dave waited for my coughing to subside to an occasional wheeze, put his hand under my chin, and lifted my head so I could see his face. "Don't make fun of me, honey. I don't like people who make fun of me. I think you should answer the sheriff's question."

If I was giong to die in this squalid room, I wouldn't do it quietly. "Goddamn coward, I don't care what you think. Why don't you take these handcuffs off and let me fight back—or are you just a fucking sissy?"

His hand clenched into a tight fist; his arm swung forward. I unsuccessfully tried to dodge it, but the blow landed on the side of my head, just above my left ear, and knocked me to the floor. Dave pulled his foot back, aiming at my head; I rolled and attempted to scramble out of his range.

The heavy boot landed in the center of my rib cage; I felt the cartilage bend and then snap. Air exploded from my lungs. The black boot moved back again and with the slow-motion, pinpoint accuracy of a place-kicker, connected with my temple. I soared through the uprights into unconsciousness.

I WAS STILL ALIVE. I opened my eyes and found myself on a dusty wooden floor, staring into an ash-filled fireplace. A surreptitious damage check wasn't encouraging. My head throbbed: possible concussion; a stabbing pain struck my chest with each breath: broken ribs; the handcuffs still encircled my wrists, all feeling was gone from my hands: possible nerve damage.

The hopelessness was smothered by a dreamlike haze that floated down over me. A long-forgotten memory pierced the mist. It was three o'clock in the morning; I was in bed, wide awake, waiting for Jeff to come home—he had been on duty for forty-eight unbroken hours—and worrying he would be gone another night. At precisely three forty-seven in the morning, I heard the tumblers in the front door locks click under his keys and listened to his footsteps, heavy with fatigue, on the steps. He tiptoed into the dark bedroom, stripped, and quietly dropped his clothes on the floor before easing into the bed, trying hard not to disturb my sleep.

I turned over, kissed his shoulder, and rubbed my hand over his bare chest. "Welcome home—I missed you. You must be exhausted."

He stroked my hair for a few moments before answering. "Yeah, but I missed you even more than you missed me."

"Have you managed to get any sleep lately?" Jeff didn't answer. I kissed his cheek and said, "I don't know how you do it."

"It's all willpower. The body always obeys if the brain commanding it is strong enough." He pulled me closer and returned my kiss. "Positive thinking. You can do almost anything if you ignore your body and don't give up when it tells you it's too tired, too sore, or too hurt to move. Wanna see how it works?"

TIME TO TEST Jeff's theory. I stifled a groan and rolled over. Price was gone. Dave was sitting in the rocking chair, drinking from a whiskey bottle, watching me. He picked up the bottle and squatted beside me.

"Hey, honey, how ya doing?" He rubbed my shoulder. "I'm real sorry I lost my temper, but it's your fault; you shouldn't have talked to me like that. I don't like it when women make fun of me. I get real mad."

His whiskey breath frightened me; I was afraid of what he could do when alcohol loosened his inhibitions. The gentle patting on my shoulder turned into a soft caress. "Why don't we try to be nice to each other?" He leaned closer and pulled me up to a sitting position. "Let's party a little." He waved the bottle and held it up to my mouth. "Want a drink?"

I stiffened and tried to move away. His fingers, which had been casually draped around my shoulders, tightened. "What's a matter? Don't you like to party? I'm just trying to be nice and you go and insult me again."

"Hey, I'm not trying to insult you; I like to party. It's just—" I looked away and stared at the floor. "I have to go to the bathroom."

"Ah honey, is that the problem? Hell, you don't have to be embarrassed." He took a swig from the bottle and carefully put it down on the floor in front of the fireplace before standing up. He easily lifted me with one hand. I started to grimace from the pain caused by the abrupt movement but managed to turn it into a shaky smile. Dave grinned, happy we were becoming friends.

We walked to a narrow door next to the sink. Dave pointed to the door and said, "Okay, it's in there. Don't take too long."

"Aren't you forgetting something?"

He frowned. "What?"

I jangled the handcuffs. "You're gonna have to let me use my hands."

"Maybe I was planning to go in there with you and pull your pants down myself."

He expected a retort; I didn't give him one. I bowed my head, stared at the floor, and bit my lower lip. "Okay honey, I'm sorry." He reached into his pocket, removed a tiny silver key, and fumbled with the manacles.

My arms swung loose. Cramped muscles in my arms and shoulders burned and ached. I shook my hands and rubbed my wrists, trying to restore the circulation. My freedom was short lived; Dave grabbed my hands and refastened the handcuffs. I wasn't surprised. He wasn't drunk enough to be completely stupid, but my objective had been accomplished—my hands were now in front of my body. I hid my satisfaction and meekly said, "This isn't necessary."

"Sorry, honey, the sheriff would kill me if he found out I let you run around without them." He opened the door and flipped the light switch. "You've got five minutes to make yourself pretty for me."

I splashed cold water on my face and shook the drops off, studiously avoiding glancing into the mirror. I didn't want to see and start counting the bruises—it would have been too upsetting. I sat on the edge of the bathtub and looked around the room. The tub was filled with empty cartons, the medicine cabinet was empty, and the window was too high and too narrow to use for an escape route.

The thin plywood door shook under Dave's fist. "Come on, honey, time's up. Don't make me come in after you."

"Okay, give me another minute." Inspiration struck. I stood on the toilet and reached for the lightbulb which swung from a wire socket. I unscrewed the bulb, waited for my eyes to adjust to the darkness, stepped down, and cracked it on the porcelain edge of the sink. Pieces of glass tinkled to the ground. I ran my finger over the jagged edge of stem and planned my attack.

I pushed the door open and stepped out. Dave, who had the whiskey bottle in hand again, stood between me and the front door; he didn't notice the lightbulb in my hand. I rushed over to him, jammed the glass into his right eye, twisted it, and dragged the stalk down his cheek. He bellowed with both pain and surprise and covered his face with his hands. I shoved him against the wall and ran through the open door.

One foot was outside on the porch when a hand caught a clump of hair and dragged me back inside the shack. I twisted and swung my clenched hands at his face; the metal of the handcuffs caught him on the side of the head just above the ear. He staggered, pushed me against the table, and moved to block my path to the doorway.

Blood oozed from the rake marks on his cheek, he touched his hand to the wound, looked down at the blood on his palm, and smiled. I shivered; blood turned him on.

He charged, I feinted to the left, and when he moved in that direction, sprinted to the right, darting to the doorway. Dave must have played tackle in high school football because my move didn't fool him; he grabbed my arm and flung me to the floor. I slid into the stand of tools near the fireplace, knocked the rack over, grabbed a black metal poker, and scrambled to my feet.

Dave laughed and said, "Okay, honey, I like to play rough. Let's see how you do against this." The knife, its long, sharp blade open, appeared in his hand. He went into a low crouch and crept toward me. "I'm going to cut you up real good, you bitch."

I didn't give him an opportunity to get close enough to carry out his threat; I swung. The poker smashed across his face, flattening his nose. Blood gushed from his nose and mouth; he slowly sank to his knees, a startled expression on his face. He toppled to the floor, convulsed once, and was still. I rolled him over, not to check his condition—I didn't care if he lived or died—but to remove the key ring from his pocket.

My hands were shaking. I took a deep breath, steadied my quaking nerves, and managed to fit the key into the lock. The handcuffs dropped to the floor. I crawled back to Dave; he was deathly still. I unsnapped the holster on his gunbelt and removed the pistol.

I ran outside—shuffled would be a more accurate description—and stood on the porch for a second. The police car was parked at the foot of the stairs, key in the ignition. Driving it back into town would be stupid and conspicuous, but I didn't have any choice. I knew I would never make it back to Dolphin Beach on foot; conserving energy was my main priority.

The ride to town was harrowing. I kept listening to the police radio, expecting to hear a warning about my escape, and fighting to keep my eyes open. The car veered off the pavement, but I jerked my head up and the car back onto the road; the adrenaline rush from the near accident kept me alert for the rest of the trip.

THE PIER WAS BUSTLING with activity. Small pools of light from the streelights illuminated the name JESSICA on the docked boat, the van parked at the foot of the gangway, and the men scurrying up and down the walkway loading bundles into the waiting vehicle. I darted between the reservoirs of darkness and stacks of cargo, attempting to get closer to the ship.

Fatigue made me careless. I didn't notice the figure hiding behind a large freight container until an iron hand grabbed my arm. "You are one dumb, stubborn bitch. I've been waiting for you. Dave missed his radio check, so I sent a couple of my men out to check up; they radioed that Dave was dead and you were gone. I knew you'd show up here." Price kept a firm grip on my arm as he pulled me down the dock to the boat.

A quiet voice broke through the darkness. "John, let her go."

We both recognized the voice. Price tightened his hold on my arm and called out, "You keep out of this, Reynolds. Go on back to your hospital and let me do my work. This ain't none of your business."

"I'm making this my business. Somebody has to stop you—what you're doing here is wrong."

"Sure." Price spat the word out from between clenched teeth. "It's easy for you to judge. You make two hundred thousand a year, got yourself a fancy house and a fancy boat. You can just pull out a credit card and buy any little toy you want. I'm only trying to make something for myself and for my family. Don't push me, Doc." He raised his gun, jabbed it into my neck, and called out, "I've got your girlfriend— and a gun."

"You're not the only one with a gun." Hugh stepped out from behind a tall pile of crates and into a small circle of light. I groaned; a hunting rifle was cradled in his arms.

Price laughed. "Now, Doc, don't you think you're going a little too far? We've known each other too long to be doing this."

"Let her go, John. You've known me long enough to understand that I mean what I'm saying. You hurt her and I'll kill you." Hugh stepped closer, well within range of the .38 in Price's hand.

Price forgot about me, all his attention on Hugh. I drove an elbow into his soft stomach, yelled a warning to Hugh, and dove behind an iron stanchion, grimacing as I landed on my battered chest. I fought off a wave of unconsciousness and lifted my head. Price was crouched in a firing stance, his gun pointed at Hugh. He called out, "Doc, I'm warning you, put that rifle down and get the hell out of here."

Hugh's answer was indistinguishable above the roaring in my ears. I didn't have much time before I lost the battle for awareness and fell into the widening pool of blackness opening beneath me. I braced myself behind the metal pillar and called out, "Price—"

I never finished my sentence. Price whirled and fired. I saw the muzzle flash, lifted Dave's police special, and concentrated on keeping my arm steady. I fired once and passed out.

SIXTEEN

Sunday

A SHADOWY FIGURE chased me. The haze was too thick; I couldn't identify my pursuer. I thrashed around, trying to escape. The figure continued to follow.

I was vaguely aware of Eileen at my side, holding my hand, uttering soothing words. I tried to warn her of the danger but the nightmare always pulled me down before I could make her understand. The vision gradually faded, and I slept peacefully.

SEVENTEEN

Monday

I WOKE UP FEELING sluggish and disoriented, the inside of my head fuzzy, my mouth dry. It was dark outside; a lamp on a table near the window threw off enough dim light for me to recognize my surroundings. I was in a hospital bed; a clear liquid dripped from an overhead IV rack and flowed through a plastic tube stuck into my right arm. I cautiously stretched and felt the pull of adhesive at the top of my chest. My fingers touched a gauze bandage as a hazy bad memory stirred.

"I've been waiting for you to wake up." The low voice from a chair next to the bed startled me into full consciousness.

"Boyd! How did you get in?" I pushed myself up and looked at him. His legs were crossed; a paper bag rested on his lap.

The tiny lamp provided enough light for me to see a grin spread across his face. "Your doctor, or should I say boyfriend, ordered your sister back to her hotel for some rest...."

Eileen was here? There were too many confusing gaps. I shook my head and forced my attention back to Boyd. "...The poor girl was exhausted. So I decided to keep you company. It was easy, the local authorities—or what's left of them—neglected to post a guard. I simply walked in and sat down." He leaned forward and tossed the bag on the bed. "Only we're not going to stay long. Get dressed."

A glimmer of light reflected off the gun in his hand; my stomach dropped. I prodded the bag and, desperately trying to keep concern from my voice, asked, "What's this, a get-well present?"

He wasn't amused. "Get dressed. It's time for you to check out."

The drugs being pumped into my arm clouded my thinking. I wanted to stall, but the most brilliant response I could manage was, "What?"

Not surprisingly, my retort didn't work. With deadly accuracy, Boyd uttered the one threat certain to work. "Get dressed or I'll ring the call button and shoot everyone who walks in here."

We looked at each other, measuring each other's resolve. He plucked the control from the table. I surrendered and mumbled, "This isn't going to work." Neither of us believed it. I opened the bag: Jeans, a red T-shirt, and white sneakers spilled out onto the bed.

I stared at them; he waved the pistol and said, "Hurry up before someone comes in. The clothes should fit; they were Amanda's. You and she were about the same size.

After that comment, no one spoke. We had nothing to say.

I jerked the intravenous needle from my arm, sat on the edge of the bed, pulled the jeans on, and struggled with the sneakers. I stood up, turned away from him, and let the hospital gown fall to the floor; the cool air on my naked back highlighted my vulnerability. I shuddered and quickly pulled the shirt over my head and exposed shoulders, ignoring the tenderness in those muscles and tendons.

Boyd stood and jammed the pistol into my ribs. I winced. He whispered in my ear, "Now listen carefully. We are going to quietly walk out of this room and out of this hospital without attracting any attention. In case you're tempted to cause a scene, remember, I'll shoot anyone who tries to stop us."

I believed him.

I MEEKLY SHUFFLED beside Boyd, fuzzy headed, worrying about the weakness in my legs and the rest of my body, not believing this was happening. I'd had enough, I was through being brave; I wanted to sink down on the floor and cry myself to sleep.

We walked through the deserted corridors and out the front door. No one tried to stop us; no one noticed our departure. A nondescript rental car was parked near the entrance. Boyd opened the door on the passenger's side, held out a set of keys, and said, "Get in; you're driving."

I reluctantly accepted the keys from his outstretched hand, slid across the seat, and fumbled the key into the ignition before asking, "Where are we going?"

He moved closer and lightly pressed the gun against my neck. I leaned forward, away from the cold metal pressing against my skin; the coldness followed. His answer was succinct. "Wherever you hid Amanda's files."

I didn't move fast enough; an unmistakable click vibrated through my spine. I flinched. Boyd chuckled; he recognized my quiver of fear and enjoyed my attempt to suppress it. "Did you recognize that sound?"

"No." Of course I did, but I wouldn't admit it.

"You disappoint me. You're not very observant; that was the sound of the safety being removed. Now you can't hear it, but I'm very gently squeezing the trigger. Aren't you afraid I might squeeze it a little too hard?"

"You really are enjoying this."

The pressure from the gun increased; it pushed my head forward until I was staring at the floor. I closed my eyes and waited. He snarled, "What did you say?" I didn't answer. Headlights from a passing car swept across the windshield. Boyd dropped the gun below the dashboard and firmly planted it in my ribs. When the car passed, he promptly brought the gun back to my head. "Well, then, don't you think it's time to start driving?"

I turned the key and started the engine; maybe I could faint and run into a tree. The pressure from the gun barrel eased. I waited to hear the click of the safey being put on—and didn't. With digital accuracy, the clock in the instrument panel read, "4:37." Which day?

Boyd was in a talkative mood; he chuckled and said, "You've caused me a lot of trouble. . . ."

"Am I supposed to apologize? Is that why you killed Amanda, because she was causing trouble?"

"I didn't have any choice. She was going to ruin my business. I wasn't about to let the company go under because Amanda couldn't deal with the pressures of business." The lack of emotion in his voice scared me more than the message it delivered.

"Business pressure? You must be kidding." The prod from the gun barrel convinced me of his seriousness. Hoping to distract him, and satisfy my curiosity, I asked, "How did you get involved with Price? Isn't cocaine outside your area of expertise?"

His soft laughter was unnerving. "I have to thank Amanda for that odd partnership. She was doing some volunteer bullshit, trying to help the town fathers bring the police department into the computer age. Price was a fast learner; he believed in the technology but he was careless. Amanda found a disk he was using for his business records; she was a true hacker, nothing was safe with her around. When she deciphered Price's unsophisticated code and read about his little business, she brought it to me. I told her I'd handle everything."

Boyd, paused, relishing his tale. "And I did handle it: I took copies to Price. He was happy to take on a silent partner. That is, after I educated him about the options. It was perfect timing; the cash infusions allowed BAJ to avoid defaulting on several short-term notes." He was quiet for a moment, then he cursed and said, "But Amanda wouldn't let it go. I put her off for six or seven months but she wouldn't leave it alone. She got suspicious and kept insisting I contact someone else."

"Then she discovered the phony reports you and Wilson had put together?"

"Damn hacker! I warned her that snooping into files would cause trouble—but she wouldn't listen. Amanda had let me take care of the financial reporting. She always signed everything without question, without even reading the reports, but suddenly she refused and wanted to see everything, go over all the figures. We had a fight about it in the office; she threatened to go to the SEC. She stormed out of the office and went home."

His voice grew louder. "Amanda was still furious when I got home. She wouldn't listen, kept accusing me of betraying her and our marriage. I followed and tried to convince her that calling the SEC would ruin the company. Then she lost her temper and inadvertently let it slip that she had made copies of my files— and the original reports. Stubborn bitch—she wouldn't tell me where they were hidden."

"And so you killed her." It wasn't a question, just a flat statement of fact.

"I didn't have any choice. It was a business decision."

"That's one hell of a business decision; Amanda was beaten and shot."

"The situation got out of control. We were in the bedroom. Amanda went crazy. She was throwing clothes into an overnight bag, yelling she wouldn't spend another night under the same roof with me. She tried to run out. I grabbed her"—Boyd's voice rose, he was still surprised by Amanda's reaction—"she bit me! I hit her once or twice."

I wanted to protest; I had seen the contusions on Amanda's face. The cold presence of the gun barrel advised me to keep silent.

"We kept a pistol in the dresser; Amanda tried to get it but I got there first. She really believed I would give up the company for her."

"You fooled me; after watching your show of grief in front of Amanda's body, I couldn't believe you were involved in her death." I allowed the bitterness I was feeling to creep into my voice. "I wanted to prove your innocence."

"I did love her—but not enough to let her destroy me. Seeing her body again was shocking. It's unfortunate that Amanda's body was discovered so soon. We all would have had an easier time if she had simply disappeared for a few weeks; there would have been a lot of publicity, but it would have died down."

His lack of remorse amazed me. I struggled to keep my voice at the same conversational tone Boyd was using, although I wanted to scream and pound my fists into his face. "Why did you bother to call me?"

Boyd shook his head ruefully. "That was the one mistake I made and I'm going to correct it tonight. I knew you had worked for that insurance company and thought I would be able to control your investigation, get the claim settled, and you out of town without too much fuss. I knew Price wouldn't interfere; he was happy to have Amanda off his back.''

The wipers squeaked across the windshield. I changed to a slightly different topic. ''Were you the mugger in the parking lot?''

''After you left my house the night Amanda's body was found, I was sure you'd go back to the hotel. But I realized I was underestimating you, that it had been a mistake to get you involved. So I went to the inn; you drove in a few minutes after I got there.''

I had to ask, ''What did you hit me with?''

''A wrench. When I discovered your briefcase was stuffed with old magazines, I decided you weren't much of a threat after all. That was my second mistake. Price didn't agree with me; he wanted to get rid of you immediately. I should have listened to him.''

He sighed. ''You and Amanda were alike. You both were too stupid, or too stubborn, to listen to reason.''

Boyd was calm, much too calm. I was feeling nervous and light-headed; my brain refused to work. I tried to shake his self-assurance. ''Price knows you killed Amanda. Don't you think he'll use this as an opportunity to get rid of an unwanted partner?''

''I'm not worried about Price.'' His voice was confident. I glanced at him; the green lights from the instrument panel shone on a satisfied face. ''You did some excellent shooting the other night. Price is dead. Everyone, including your bright sister, thinks Price killed Amanda to protect his drug business.''

Dave and Price dead; the thought made me nauseous. I sternly ordered myself, ''Don't think about them, focus on the situation," and calmly said, "I know what happened."

"You made one mistake. Dear Jennifer is a horror-movie fan; she went to the midnight show at the mall on Thursday night, came out of the theater, and saw you stuffing a bulging pack into the back of your fancy car. After she told me, I took a good look around my office and Amanda's too."

He laughed softly. "You really should stop smoking; it's not good for your health. I found a fresh cigarette butt in Amanda's garbage and scratches on my desk. I knew you found the information Amanda was threatening to take to the SEC and contacted Price. Once again, I underestimated you; I thought Price would be able to persuade you to give him the file. Where did you find it?"

Boyd didn't wait for an answer. He continued. "I waited around the hospital, playing the concerned friend and waiting for a chance to get to you. My patience was rewarded; the perfect opportunity presented itself when your sister finally gave in and went back to her hotel to sleep. I could have killed you right away, but I didn't. First I want you to return the information you stole from me."

Not sure if I was trying to convince Boyd or myself, I said, "You're not going to get away with this."

He laughed; the sound grated on my nerves. "I've been hoping to hear you say that; I knew you would. Blaine dear, don't you understand? Everyone is satisfied. Price killed my wife because she stumbled upon the drug ring he was operating. You are going to be hailed as a martyr for the anti-drug movement; you broke up a huge cocaine operation—one of the largest hauls in the country—and died in service of the 'Just Say No' people. Maybe one of the networks will do a docudrama about your life. No one suspects me, not even the insurance company. They're expediting my claim; I should have a check in a few days. I'm the only person who knows the truth." He chuckled again. "And I don't have any intention of confessing."

"But—"

"But you know. Is that what you were going to say?" Patiently, as if explaining the rules of a simple game to a child, Boyd said, "No, I'm not worried about you. You'll be dead too. You're going to commit suicide."

"No one will believe I killed myself." I spoke with conviction I didn't feel. "Eileen won't believe it. There will be an investigation. It won't take long for them to take a good look at you."

"Wrong again." He chuckled. "I had a long, earnest conversation with Eileen earlier today. Your sister is very concerned about you. You've been so depressed lately. Eileen is also feeling guilty about adding to your stress by insisting on breaking up the firm." His tone was nonchalant. "Sorry, Blaine, I don't think the investigation will be too thorough. You realized you killed two people, got depressed, walked out of the hospital in the middle of the night, went back to your hotel room, got drunk, and killed yourself." The gun barrel sunk deeper into my neck. "How does that sound?"

I gripped the steering wheel harder, and determined to keep any trace of panic from my voice, quietly said, "I don't drink."

"Amanda mentioned your drinking problem. She was so proud of you; she told me about your struggle to stay sober. Don't worry; people will understand. You're only human. You've been under a great deal of physical and emotional stress ever since you arrived in Dolphin Beach. Tonight you're going to succumb to it and fall off the wagon..."

The little voice inside my head said, "Don't antagonize him." But the word slipped from between my clenched teeth before I could stop it. "Bastard."

Boyd chuckled and finished the sentence I had interrupted. "...and die."

We finished the ride in silence.

BOYD LOCKED the door of the suite. With one hand he slipped the chain through the slot and carefully tested the knob to be sure it was secure. His other hand kept a firm grip on my arm, not that a firm grip was necessary. I was panting, trying to recover from the exertion of climbing the stairs, and cursing the drugs the hospital had pumped into my system.

He lunged at me, spun me around, and sharply twisted my arm behind my back. Pain shot through my shoulder and ribs. Boyd increased the force and said, "Where are those papers?"

I clenched my teeth, determined to hide the extent of my debility from him. "What makes you think—"

He wrenched my arm higher; another sharper spasm of pain shot through my body, abruptly ending my defiant speech. Resistance wasn't going to work. I gasped, "In the bedroom closet."

We took a quick, uncomfortable stroll down the hallway. Boyd used one hand to steadily push the gun against my head; the other hand continued the relentless pressure on my arm. He stopped in the bedroom doorway, pushed me, and watched dispassionately as I stumbled into the room. I caught myself on the edge of the bed and looked at Boyd. He calmly said, "Get the file."

The lack of emotion scared me—Boyd had made another business decision. The end justifies the means: The business must be saved, regardless of the cost....

I slowly walked to the closet, wishing I'd packed a backup weapon, wondering what I would do when I got there. Frantic pounding on the outside door stopped me. Eileen's unmistakable voice called, "Blaine! Are you in there?"

"Give it up, Boyd; it's all over."

He raised the pistol.

I held out my hands, motioning for him to stop. "Listen to me, put the gun down. Don't make it worse."

"No. I won't let you destroy everything."

The door crashed open. Boyd looked down the hallway at the intruders and then turned back to me. He raised the pistol and pointed it at my chest.

The books and movies talk about a person's life passing before their eyes. It's not true; there wasn't enough time to relive anything. Resignation settled over me—I knew he was going to shoot and I knew I couldn't avoid the bullet.

He fired.

The impact flung me to the carpet. I landed on my back and lay still, puzzled by the absence of pain. Another shot boomed in the room but I was too weak to lift my head. A half dozen people crowded into the bedroom, and Eileen pushed them aside. She knelt beside me, clutched my hand, and told me I would be fine. I tried to answer but my mouth wouldn't follow the instructions from my brain. The room was growing dark and cold; I began to shiver. Eileen turned and yelled something to the men milling around the room.

From a distance, I watched one of the men rip a blanket from the bed and spread it across my body. The blanket didn't help; my shivering intensified. Eileen was talking, but I couldn't understand her words. I moved farther away and watched two paramedics rush into the room and open their cases of equipment. The noise faded to silence; darkness fell over the room.

I WAS IN a tunnel without any light. The darkness was complete; I couldn't even see my hand when I held it up in front of my eyes. And it was so cold; I was trembling and shaking in the frigid air.

A door at the end of the tunnel opened, flooding the passageway with an incandescent light, burning my eyes. I shielded them and trotted to the door, curious to see what lay beyond it.

A silhouette of a man, backlighted by the radiant light, stepped into the doorway. I squinted to see his face; he held out a hand and motioned for me to hurry. I hesitated, unsure of his identity. He beckoned again and called my name.

It was Jeff! I sprinted down the long tunnel, afraid he would disappear before I could reach him.

Faint, easy-to-ignore voices called my name. Their message was garbled. I disregarded them and concentrated on reaching Jeff. The voices grew louder and more insistent, swelling to a loud chorus roaring my name, calling me back. I stopped to listen; the chorus faded to a solitary, plaintive voice. It was Eileen. I couldn't move, paralyzed by the agony in her voice.

Jeff said, "Blaine?" I turned for one last look down the dark tunnel. Eileen was sobbing, calling my name and fighting the two men who were trying to pull her away from my body. Her pain made me cry.

I made my choice. I walked to the light, to Jeff. I was close enough to touch him, embrace him, kiss him when he stopped me. His hand gently brushed my cheek. He pushed a damp strand of hair from my face and said, "Blaine, go back. You're not ready—it's not your time."

"No!" Tears streamed down my cheeks. I shouted, "No!—Jeff, don't leave me alone again!" He wouldn't listen. He turned, walked into the light, and firmly closed the door between us. I stood alone, sobbing, shouting his name, and pleading for his return. The darkness engulfed me.

EIGHTEEN

Thursday

THREE DAYS PASSED without leaving any vestige of thoughts, memories, hopes, or dreams. I opened my eyes and found Eileen slumped in a chair next to my hospital bed, watching streams of raindrops flow down the window. She had the rumpled, weary air of a stranded traveler, forced to spend a sleepless night squirming on the plastic seats in an airport lounge. Tension and fatigue radiated from her body.

I wanted to say a few comforting words, but my heroic intentions vanished when I opened my mouth. After dragging a parched tongue over dry lips, I croaked, "I want to go home..."

Startled, she rose and leaned over the bed, a tangle of tubes and monitor wires preventing her embrace. She sank back in the chair and covered her face with trembling hands. Anguish flooded her voice. "Blaine, I'm so sorry. This"—she waved her hand over the bed—"never should have happened. If I hadn't been so pigheaded, I would have listened to you. Instead, I listened to the complaints and didn't question the motives of the people complaining. I was so ready to believe their accusations. And then I said those dreadful things about not trusting you...."

Eileen looked at me, her eyes puffy and bloodshot. "I was wrong. Even if CIG decided they didn't like the way you were conducting your investigation, I should have told them to go to hell. I should have supported you; you're my sister."

"Stop it." I stared into red-rimmed, green eyes. "Stop feeling guilty. You didn't do anything wrong. Besides, I knew you wouldn't dissolve the company—who would put up with your lousy temper?" Eileen started to answer, but I cut her off. "What happened? How did you get here?"

A wan smile flashed across Eileen's face but never reached her eyes. "They kept trying to make me leave, but I wouldn't go. Not after last time—I let Don and the doctors talk me into leaving and look what happened."

"The result would have been the same, or worse. Boyd was determined; he wouldn't have been dissuaded by your presence." I fought the urge to drift back into unconsciousness and said, "So tell me what happened."

"Dr. Reynolds decided to look in on you before he left for the evening and discovered an empty bed; he made another frantic phone call to me. Don and I were in the bar at Harbour House having a drink with some of the detectives when he called. We went to check your room and broke in. Then we heard a gunshot." She stopped, took a deep breath, and said, "You were on the floor, bleeding. Boyd was standing over you, pointing the gun at your head."

Eileen stared past me, lost in the memory of the scene she was describing. I grabbed her hand, squeezed it, and said, "Hey, I'm okay. What happened to Boyd?"

She hesitated, torn over whether to protect me or to answer my questions. After an almost imperceptible pause, she said, "You've missed a few days. Let me bring you up to date."

Eileen held my hand and began a slow narration, patiently stopping each time I fell asleep, resuming the narrative each time I woke up and said, "Go on."

"Today's Thursday. Dr. Reynolds, Hugh, called us last Friday night. We had just gone to bed—Don's flight was late. Hugh's emergency at the hospital was a false alarm. Price was having you followed and made the emergency call to Reynolds so they could hijack you when you left the restaurant. Hugh went back to the restaurant, but you had already left. The waitress told him some convoluted tale about tides, fishing boats, and how you practically ran out of the restaurant to go fishing. Fortunately, the story made sense to him. He discovered your Porsche in the inn parking lot and your room empty and really started to worry. When the valet told Hugh that a policeman had driven your car back, he called me—my home number was on some insurance forms you filled out in his office."

I smiled; Eileen noticed and raised her eyebrows. I said, "And everybody makes fun of me for being overprotective about the Porsche."

She nodded. "Okay, I won't make fun anymore. In the future you can park that car anywhere you'd like and I won't say a word. Reynolds repeated your dinner conversation; my imagination filled in the gaps. Don and I called in a lot of favors; he got someone's corporate jet, and we flew down immediately. I convinced the state attorney general and the state police to meet us. We all arrived at the pier just as you shot Price."

"Boyd told me Price died. Is that true or is the sheriff still lurking in the shadows?"

"Boyd wasn't lying."

I closed my eyes and turned away, clenching my jaws to hold down the bile rising in my throat. Eileen's relentless monotone continued. "Hugh tried to administer first aid. It didn't work; Price died. The boat was filled with cocaine, one of the largest shipments ever intercepted in the country." As an afterthought Eileen said, "I wish you had been able to make me listen to you."

I mumbled, "Quit blaming yourself." Eileen, who was hoping I would fall asleep, didn't answer. I opened my eyes, looked at her and impatiently asked, "What happened to Boyd?"

Her eyes narrowed; she was censoring her answer. I pushed myself up with an elbow and, ignoring the pain in my chest, said in the most menacing tone I could managed, "Eileen?"

Her eyes focused on the door, she switched her gaze to the window, and addressed the rain streaking down the glass. "We heard a shot and ran into the bedroom. Boyd was standing over you, aiming at your head. He looked at us and shot himself. ... He died in the ambulance.''

Amanda was dead. Davis was dead. Dave was dead. Price was dead. Boyd was dead. The list was too long; I stopped listening and let my tired eyelids close.

Eileen gently touched my shoulder. ''Blaine, don't fall asleep on me now.'' The urgency in Eileen's voice forced my eyes open. ''Price mentioned Amanda's files before he died, and Amanda's attorney has been insisting they're important. Where are they?''

''No files . . . computer disks. Amanda made them; they describe the fake reports Boyd and his accountant created. It was an interesting scam they set up.'' I gave Eileen a quick summary of the information Amanda had left me.

Eileen smiled. ''Disks. That explains the computer in your room. I didn't think you had suddenly decided to use your vacation to enter the computer age. Where are they?''

''In the mail.'' I described my daily routine of packing my treasures into manila envelopes and dropping them in a mailbox. ''Corny, but it worked. People were getting into my suite without any trouble; I couldn't leave anything important there. Talk to Jim, the night manager. He should be holding a package for me.''

She stood up. ''About a dozen people are pacing up and down the corridor, waiting to hear your answer; I'll be right back.''

I was asleep before she left the room.

NINETEEN

MY HOSPITAL STAY dragged on for two slow weeks. Eileen maintained her bedside vigil for half of those weeks; she flew back to New York only after being satisfied I was healing properly and receiving appropriate care. Long, twice-a-day telephone calls replaced her constant bedside presence. I was cranky, lonely, and restless; Eileen's calls were a welcome respite from the strenuous physical therapy regimen and the boredom of hospital routine.

Release day finally arrived. The Porsche had been shipped home, first-class plane tickets had been sent by courier, and hospital bills were reconciled. I settled myself into the leather airplane seat, glad Eileen had efficiently orchestrated my return to New York City.

The trip started with a good omen; the plane took off on time. I stayed awake long enough to watch the bright green land, cut by angry slashes of red clay soil, fade to gray as we gained altitude. We reached thirty thousand feet, the ground was completely hidden by the cloud cover, and the flight attendants started to serve drinks. Nap time. I pulled down the window shade and closed my eyes. It was the last time I would see Dolphin Beach.

During those two weeks in the hospital Hugh had consistently, and successfully, avoided me. With perfect timing, he came in only when I was asleep or the room was crowded with doctors, nurses, or officials asking questions. Their questions were all answered, but my questions about why Hugh was avoiding me went unanswered, until yesterday...

I was in bed, propped up against the pillows, staring at the television. Morning talk shows faded into game shows, soap operas, late afternoon talk shows, and the early evening news. Not a word sank in through the numbness; I was content to stare at the tiny figures, welcoming the distraction of the inane dialogue and bellowing laugh tracks.

Hugh walked into the room as the local evening news broadcast was beginning. Without saying a word, he busied himself with a brief examination, a rather indifferent one according to my experienced eye. I took deep breaths on command like a good patient, wondering why I was being treated like a stranger. Hugh scribbled some notes on the chart he carried under his arm and closed it with a snap, abandoning all pretense of his visit being prompted by medical concerns. I looked at him; he refused to meet my eyes and said, "So you're going to be discharged tomorrow. Are you going back to New York right away?"

"Yes. I'm flying back as soon as you doctors let me out of here. Eileen, bless her organizing soul, arranged everything. She was probably afraid I'd take off and try to finish this vacation instead of going home." Hoping to achieve a bantering tone, I asked, "Do you have any last words of medical wisdom?"

He wrapped the stethoscope around his neck, sat on the edge of the bed, and said, "You know, that bullet went through your lung. This would be a perfect time for you to stop smoking."

Give up smoking? My plans for release day had "Buy a pack of cigarettes" in the number one spot. I smiled and sat up to take Hugh's hand. He flinched and moved out of my reach.

Surprised by his reaction, I awkwardly said, "Hugh, what's wrong? You haven't come near me unless you have a dozen people with you. I'm leaving in the morning, I wanted to thank you for saving my life—"

"Why? So you can get yourself killed next week or next month?" His voice cracked, "I hate guns, I've lost too many patients with gunshot wounds. The rifle I had belonged to my daddy, he gave it to me before he died. I clean it every Saturday, just like he did, but I never shot it. I never tried to use it, not until the other night. I was ready to kill another man. That scared me."

"And I did kill him. Is that why you've been avoiding me?"

"Yes, that's part of the reason," Hugh sighed and finally looked at me, "I've been doing a lot of thinking."

I decided to make it easier for him. I sat back against the pillows and asked, "Is this the big brush-off scene? If it is, don't go through all the trouble, I understand.''

''This isn't a brush-off, not unless you want it to be.'' Hugh stared at a spot on the wall behind my head and rushed into his confession. ''I stayed away because I've been too ashamed of myself to face you. I knew Price was corrupt; everyone in town knew that. No one did anything about it. I didn't—''

''How many times can a man turn his head, pretending he just doesn't see?''

Hugh looked at me, a blank expression on his face. ''What?''

''Bob Dylan, 'Blowing In The Wind.' ''

''Something like that. It was easier to ignore the situation; I took the easy way out.''

''You didn't know about the drugs, did you?'' Hugh shook his head. I shrugged and asked, ''So, what were you supposed to do?''

''I didn't tell you that Price was a bad cop; I just tried to talk you into giving up. When the paramedics brought you in the hospital, you were almost...'' Hugh cleared his throat and finally looked at me. ''I realized how wrong I had been. I'm sorry. Don't go back to New York tomorrow. Stay with me for a week or two, finish your vacation. The rest would be good for you.''

The offer was tempting, but I couldn't stay. I had to get back to work—vacations don't agree with me.

EPILOGUE

IT TOOK DYING, or almost dying, to bring me back to life. Even after all this time, I'm still not sure what happened to me that night in Dolphin Beach and I've never discussed it with anyone. Deep inside my heart, when I dare to be honest with myself, I believe my trip down that long, dark tunnel was real. I also believe Jeff sent me back to life; it's an awareness I carry with me every day—I was sent back to life.

Hard Luck

A Cat Marsala Mystery

Barbara D'Amato

First Time in Paperback

HIGH STAKES

Chicago journalist Cat Marsala has just begun her assignment on the state lottery when murder falls into the picture— literally—as a lottery official takes a leap in the middle of the multistate lottery conference.

Suicide... or murder? It's curious to Cat—and to the police— that the guy took his mighty plunge right before his meeting with her. Especially curious since he'd hinted at some great exposé material, like "misappropriation" of lottery funds.

"Cat Marsala is one of the most appealing new sleuths to come along in years."
— *Nancy Pickard*

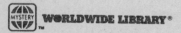